Let your brother go. He's dead. And I'm alive.

There was a ruthless truth in what Annabel Parker had said.

The hell of it was he still wanted her. And he'd have her. Why not? She'd handed him the choice of passion with her if he let his passion for truth go. More might come out of it than she planned on giving him. If he walked away he'd be left burning with frustration on every level.

A grim laugh graveled from his throat. If nothing else, he'd have a sexual experience worth having. At least he'd be satisfied on that score.

They were both booked in for six more days at this resort. Six nights. He'd take them and no more, he decided. He was not about to lose his soul to Annabel Parker. He could be every bit as ruthless as she when it came to self-preservation.

Initially a French/English teacher, **EMMA DARCY** changed careers to computer programming before marriage and three lively sons settled her into community life. Very much a people person, always interested in relationships, she finds the challenge of creating new stories highly addictive. Her first novel for MIRA Books will be published in October 1997. THE SECRETS WITHIN is Emma Darcy at her most daring.

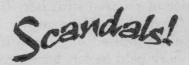

Have you heard the latest?
Get ready for the next outrageous Scandal
A VERY PUBLIC AFFAIR (#1912)
by
Sally Wentworth
All will be revealed in October 1997

EMMA DARCY

Seducing the Enemy

Harlequin Books

TORONTO • NEW YORK • LONDON
AMSTERDAM • PARIS • SYDNEY • HAMBURG
STOCKHOLM • ATHENS • TOKYO • MILAN
MADRID • WARSAW • BUDAPEST • AUCKLAND

ISBN 0-373-11906-2

SEDUCING THE ENEMY

First North American Publication 1997.

CHAPTER ONE

HE'S dead.

The thought gave Annabel Parker intense satisfaction as she reread the killing summary of her article for the *Australian National*. She'd nailed Barry Wolfe to the wall this time. The long-time powerbroker in state politics and current finance minister couldn't dodge these facts and figures. No need to add another word to what she'd written. Everything pointed directly to him.

Annabel smiled over the headline she'd chosen—"Pattern of Corruption." There was a purity in patterns that couldn't be obscured by personalities. The flamboyant and charismatic Barry Wolfe had fooled the public for too many years. The man oozed charm. One flash of his raffish grin and they fell in a heap, believing him, forgiving him, loving him. Accountability was well overdue.

She didn't have the smoking gun, but the overwhelming bank of circumstantial evidence should land him straight into the courtroom of the commission into corruption. He'd need more than his handsome face and silver tongue to extract himself from that legal body. For one thing, the presiding judge was not a susceptible female.

It would be interesting to see if Daniel Wolfe, Q.C., would step in to defend his brother. The two men were poles apart, one embracing the law, the other holding it in contempt. The famous barrister had made his reputation winning unwinnable cases. It was said he could turn black into white. Nevertheless, Annabel very much doubted that even the highly skilled and formidable Daniel from the Sydney law courts could rescue his brother from the lions and resurrect a political career that was so deeply set in mire.

He's dead.

Annabel was certain of it.

Having spent months following the money trails of dubious deals, and all this evening making every word count, she felt a sense of completion as she stapled the pages of the final printout together and locked the political dynamite in her filing cabinet.

Working from home had its advantages, but it meant the article would not be handed to her editor until tomorrow. Nevertheless, it was easy to imagine his elation over breaking such a high-ranking scandal. He'd be clearing the decks to use it for maximum impact.

Selling newspapers was not important to Annabel. Getting rid of corruption was. People like Barry Wolfe lined their own pockets while they sold their country down the drain. A complete shake-up was needed in the finance department. Ideally, her article would help to clean up the system of management and put some economic sanity back into the handling of public funding.

She was about to switch off the computer when her desk phone rang. The clock read ten forty-two.

The late hour of the call brought an automatic frown, an unease.

Isabel...

Instinct identified her twin sister as the caller even before Annabel lifted the receiver. Her sixth sense picked up trouble, big trouble!

"Anna..." A desperate, frantic cry.

"Yes. What's the problem, Izzie?" The automatic adoption of their childhood names for each other affirmed the special link that had always been theirs.

"He's dead!"

The echo of her own thoughts rocked Annabel momentarily.

"He's dead, and I don't know what to do."

Panic coming at her in waves. Annabel steadied her whirling mind. It had to be Isabel's husband. "Neil?"

"Oh, God! Neil will throw me out. He'll take our children from me. He'll never let me see them again." Hysteria breaking into wild sobbing.

Not Neil. Not family. A victim of a car accident? "Isabel!" She shouted to snap her sister back to the immediate problem. "Who is dead?"

It sobered her. "You'll despise me." Fear shaking through the evasion.

"Nonsense! I can't help you if you don't give me the facts. Where are you? What's happened? Who's dead?"

The firm demands succeeded in cutting through the emotional chaos at the other end of the line. Deep shuddering breaths, then, "I... I'm at a motel near you. The...the Northgate. We're in room twenty-eight.''

Shock. Her straightlaced twin with a man in a motel? Neil Mason would certainly go off his brain. An adulterous wife would make a mockery of the family values he espoused for his political platform.

''It must have been a heart attack,'' Isabel cried. ''I wanted to call it off. We were arguing and he...he clutched his chest and collapsed. I gave him mouth-to-mouth resuscitation. I tried everything I could think of.''

''How long since he collapsed?''

''Fifteen, twenty minutes...''

''You're sure he's dead?''

''I couldn't get anything going again. No pulse. No breathing. Nothing. He was dead within seconds.''

Too late for paramedics to revive him now. Dead was dead, and discovery could wait. It wouldn't make any difference to the man. The need to protect her twin surged to the fore.

''Get out of there, Izzie. Walk to my apartment— it's safer than catching a cab—and I'll take you home,'' she instructed strongly, seeing no sense in her sister's life being destroyed when there was no possibility of saving her lover.

Another burst of sobbing. ''It's no use. Someone took a photograph of us. I can be identified. Will you come and...and stand by me, Anna? I can't face it alone.''

Annabel's heart sank. ''He's a married man?'' It was all she could think of—a wife having her husband trailed by a private investigator, taking a photograph to prove infidelity. If she was the vindictive type, the fatal affair could blow up into one hell of a scandal with Neil Mason's wife involved.

"No. He's not married," came the gulping reply.

"Then why the photograph?" It made no sense.

"I don't know. I was frightened. I wanted to leave. We had a fight. He laughed at me, saying one bell was as good as another. Whatever that meant. It all turned ugly and then—then..."

Some kind of set-up? Blackmail? Someone out to tarnish Neil's puritanical policies? Or... A weird feeling of premonition crawled down Annabel's spine.

The motel was only a few streets from where she lived in North Sydney. Her sister lived right across the city at Brighton-Le-Sands. With so many motels stretching over that distance, why come anywhere near her?

"Who's your dead Romeo, Izzie?"

"I know you thought he was crooked, Anna, but he was so—so..."

"Who?" she asked, the premonition jagging into her heart. *One bell as good as another*. Isabel, Annabel, identical twin sisters, the same rippling cloud of distinctive red hair, green eyes, every physical feature such a close match. A photograph of either one of them could be mistaken for the other. "Tell me his name. Now!" she commanded tersely.

"Barry Wolfe."

CHAPTER TWO

"He's *dead*?"

Shock and incredulity forced the question, even though Daniel Wolfe had no reason to disbelieve the journalist on the other end of the line. Jack Mitchell was a reputable and reliable reporter, not given to sensationalism for the sake of it. In interviews Daniel had given him on various court cases he had always quoted accurately. The call was a friendly gesture, a warning of what was to come. It just seemed inconceivable that Barry was dead.

"It happened at the Northgate Motel." Information delivered matter-of-factly, leaving no room for doubt. "It's not far from where you are at Neutral Bay."

Daniel took a deep breath, trying to get himself on an even keel. "Yes. I know it." A long, Spanish-style complex leapt to mind. Near a set of lights.

"He was with a woman. I don't know the details yet, but he wouldn't be the first guy who screwed himself to death, Daniel."

"A heart attack?" Still incredible. Barry was a fitness freak. He'd run in the Sydney city-to-surf race only a fortnight ago. Being in good shape—attractive shape—was important to him.

"Sounds like it. There's been no suggestion of

foul play. The motel manager notified the cops of his death. I'm on my way to the Northgate now. It's big news, Daniel. You'll be getting other calls.''

"Yes." As the other high-profile member of the family, he would certainly be a target for comment. "Thanks for...for preparing me."

"Sorry to give you the news, but there it is."

"Decent of you."

He put the receiver down slowly, his mind dazedly groping towards accepting the facts. His finger pressed the button activating the answering machine. Better not take any more calls until he'd thought this through.

Barry dead. At only forty-two. The prime of life.

Daniel shook his head. There had always been something Peter Pan-ish about Barry, a perky, irrepressible vitality that could skate out of any trouble, a devil-may-care grin on his face, a daring twinkle in his eyes. It was almost impossible to imagine death catching him. It must have sneaked up on him, without warning. That it should come while he was with a woman... Daniel grimaced. *Whose* woman was the question.

It had to be a woman who was publicly attached to another man. Why else a motel? Barry's tomcatting had always been indiscriminate. No respect whatsoever for wedding rings. Nothing he did on the sexual front could surprise Daniel, but these circumstances would almost inevitably lead to a muckraking scandal.

His father would hate it.

Barry's mother would probably laugh and say it

was a fitting climax for the dear boy's life, taking his pleasure to the end. Having been through four husbands, Marlene was enjoying a succession of toy boys and would undoubtedly fancy going out the same way.

Daniel didn't anticipate deep grieving from either parent. Vexation and titillation respectively. A sad reflection of Barry's place in their lives. It wasn't fair, Daniel thought, as he'd often thought over the years, seeing the careless treatment of Barry by his self-indulgent mother and the cool toleration dealt out to him by his father. It wasn't Barry's fault he had been a mistake to both of them. Though there was no denying he'd developed plenty of faults of his own along the way to this final, fatal night.

Nevertheless, it felt wrong to do nothing when all the vultures would be gathering to pick at the juicy bits attached to Barry's death. He should be there, at the motel, monitoring what was happening, insisting on some dignity to the proceedings. Death was so damned naked, respecting nothing. Maybe he could do something for the woman, as well. No one deserved to be stripped in public.

The answering machine beeped an incoming call. Daniel left it to play itself out, striding quickly out of his private library office where he'd been studying the brief for tomorrow's court appearance. He knew what he needed to know for the line of questioning he'd chosen. Tomorrow's work could wait upon tomorrow. Tonight he owed to Barry. Someone should care, and there was no one else.

It was getting on towards midnight by the time

Daniel forced his way through the bedlam outside the motel, police cars, television news vans, reporters and photographers pressing for whatever story angles they could grab, not to mention a crowd of curious spectators drawn by the unusual activity. Daniel headed for the police cordon keeping people from the ambulance, which was backed up to a room midway along one of the motel's residential wings. Having identified himself to one of the officers, he was immediately escorted inside.

The next ten minutes were a blur. The only thing that really registered was the certain knowledge Barry was truly gone. The life that had made the person he knew so well was not there any more. The ambulance men wheeled the stretcher away, and under Daniel's watchful eye, a proper decorum was maintained in the immediate vicinity until the departure of the ambulance could be effected.

The woman had been moved to an adjoining room. Daniel was asked by the police officer in charge if he would like to hear her statement, which was about to be taken. Determined to know the worst and deal with it as best he could, he quickly agreed.

His heart plummeted when he saw who the woman was. Isabel Mason! The supposedly purer-than-snow wife of the most vocal family-values politician in the current government. Barry was certainly going out with a bang! This scandal would reach epic proportions.

It amazed him that she looked so composed, sitting calmly at a table, sipping at a cup of tea or coffee. He would have expected her to be in floods of tears, or at least showing some signs of distress. Her hand wasn't even trembling. A policewoman sat by her, but it seemed to Daniel no comfort was required.

"Miss Parker?"

Isabel Mason looked directly at the chief officer, as though it was she being addressed.

"Are you ready now?"

She *was* being addressed! Daniel frowned. Did she think she could get away with giving a false name?

"Yes." A crisp consent. She glanced pointedly at Daniel, clearly wanting him identified.

"The deceased's brother, Daniel Wolfe," the police officer obliged. Then with an introductory wave, "Miss Annabel Parker."

Annabel Parker? The journalist who'd been snapping at Barry's heels over his dubious dealings? She was a dead ringer for Isabel Mason!

Then she looked at him directly, and twin bolts of green fire zapped his brain. It was a fierce mental blast, hurling him off into a far space where he existed only as some infinitesimal speck, too insignificant to claim her attention. Absolutely no help was required by this woman. Having disposed of him, she returned her gaze to the chief police officer and started her account of her meeting with Barry.

Daniel sat down. She certainly wasn't Isabel Mason. She had the same glorious red hair, rippling down to swirl around her shoulders. And the same features, though there was something stronger about the bone structure of her face, a cleaner, sharper definition. The most striking difference came from within. This woman's mind had a brutal force that was light-years removed from the soft, pliable femininity he'd seen emanating from Neil Mason's wife.

He watched her mouth as she spoke. Words were shaped with precision, her lips firmly sculptured, not a trace of quivering uncertainty. He listened to what she said, fascinated by the cool, clear logic of her story. Brick by brick, she laid a convincing foundation for her convincing conclusion. It was a formidable performance.

He'd no sooner thought the word *performance* than she looked at him again, another stunning blaze that dared him to challenge anything she said. It promised she'd wipe the floor with him.

Daniel said nothing. He was too intrigued to want to do anything but watch her. She was magnificent. A unique entity. He'd never met anyone like her.

She wore black, a ribbed sweater that moulded superbly rounded breasts. A short, narrow skirt revealed long, shapely legs, sexily emphasised in black tights. She was tall, a good fit for him. What would it feel like to be entwined with a woman who was fired with an incredible store of secret energy? That could be an adventure worth having.

He'd like to know the rest of her, too.

She had everyone else bluffed.

Barry couldn't have done it better himself, and he'd been a genius at sliding out of sticky spots. The story was completely sanitised of sex. The only scandal emerging from it would be a political one, and that had been brewing anyway.

Bravo, Annabel Parker!

The truth—whatever it was—was successfully skittled.

Daniel knew she was lying.

CHAPTER THREE

FREEDOM...

Annabel heaved a contented sigh. It was marvellous not to be constantly on guard. She revelled in the sense of tranquillity that flowed from this beautiful place in far north Queensland, thousands of kilometres away from the frenzy of scandals still breaking in Sydney. From this corner of her cabin, where only an insect screen separated her from the primitive splendour on view, she could gaze out over the lush rainforest to the sea and feel blissfully removed from the corrupt touch of mankind.

It was an illusion, of course. The cabin was part of a wilderness tourist resort built to capitilise on precisely this feeling. Nevertheless, great care had been taken to nestle it into the environment. None of the buildings was intrusive. They didn't spoil. This was the only place on the planet where two world heritage wonders met—the Great Barrier Reef and the Daintree Rainforest—and the Coconut Beach Rainforest Resort offered the experience of both within a context of personal comfort.

The only sounds were made by birds and animals. No television or telephones in the guest accommodation. No newspapers. Even the people here went about their activities in a quiet and unobtrusive manner. Peace...sheer heaven to Annabel.

The weeks since Barry Wolfe's death had been hectic and highly stressful. Thankfully, that was all behind her—the frantic substitution of herself for Isabel at the motel on that fatal night, the tension involved in giving a formal statement to the police, the seemingly endless inquisition by the media. Annabel felt she had more than earned this escape from the pressure of having to perform.

Izzie was surely safe now. They could both relax. If the photograph taken of her twin sister and Barry Wolfe entering the motel room could have disproved Annabel's account of events, it would have surfaced when the news was hot. Or been used for blackmail before this. The danger was gone. Neil Mason would never find out that his wife had flirted with infidelity. Barry Wolfe was dead and buried.

Annabel ruefully reflected that she hadn't wished him dead in the physical sense, yet she couldn't regret his passing. The world was a cleaner place for it. Getting cleaner by the day down in Sydney, where the cover-ups were unravelling without any assistance from her.

Maybe it had been overly squeamish of her not to capitalise on the article she had written. Her editor had almost been frothing at the mouth for it. She'd worked so hard at putting the Barry Wolfe corruption story together, and it had probably been unprofessional not to go through with it, yet when it came to the point of deciding on publication the

morning after his death, it had felt like overkill—
brutal, unfeeling, unnecessary.

The man was dead. Not only that, she and her
sister had been caught up in the circumstances sur-
rounding his death. It made it all too personal,
somehow. Besides, there was no moral gain in a
public demolition of Barry Wolfe's career when
that career had died with him.

Definitely overkill.

She didn't need that kind of professional kudos.
She had only ever wanted the truth to come out so
the corruption would come to an end. Which it had.

Although she had held back the damning article,
she had been pressed into referring to her work on
it, with the media demanding the reason for her
meeting with Barry Wolfe in what was perceived
as a clandestine manner. That in itself, plus details
of her research, had raised enough questions to trigger an investigation.

Ironically, the finance minister's death had ex-
posed his cronies in corruption. Without his strong
front to protect them, they were scrambling to explain their activities to the new minister, who was
demanding accountability in no uncertain terms.

But Annabel didn't have to think about any of it
any more. The desired result had been achieved.
She could breathe in this gloriously fresh air and
simply enjoy herself.

Twilight was bleaching the sea of colour. It was
time to walk down to the Long House near the
beach for dinner. Although the paths were ad-
equately lit, she preferred to go before darkness fell,

to savour the ambience of the forest around her in its softer evening mood.

Her cabin was situated high on the hill, perched on stilts to counter the steep gradient. When she had arrived yesterday, the porter had commented on its isolation, wondering if it worried her. Annabel smiled over his concern as she locked the door behind her and started down the steps from the porch. Being left alone was precisely what she wanted.

The path that served her cabin also wound around the next, which was seven or eight metres distant and at a slightly lower level. Yesterday it had been vacant. The door opened as she was about to pass by, drawing her curiosity. New guests or one of the staff?

The man who emerged blasted her light-heartedness. Recognition was instant, rocking her with shock. Her feet faltered to a halt. The smile lingering on her lips sagged into a gasp of dismay. Her mind reeled against accepting the reality of his physical presence here.

"Good evening," he said, offering the casual grace of a fellow guest, lending substance to the form, chasing away any chance he was a mirage.

Daniel Wolfe!

Barry Wolfe's brother!

In the cabin next to hers!

Annabel couldn't believe in coincidence. A convulsive shiver ran down her spine as she remembered him sitting in the motel room while her statement was taken down by the police, watching her recount how and when his brother had died and what she'd done about it. He hadn't said a word, but his eyes had drilled into her with riveting concentration, raising the eerie sense that she was the accused in a witness box.

The fire in her belly to see real justice done had surged into a blaze of challenge that seared a silent but highly electric path between them. *Not me, my friend.* Her eyes had spoken in fierce rebuttal of anything he could do to her. *You won't get to me any more than your brother did.*

He hadn't then.

She hadn't let him.

But now?

"Good evening," she returned, struggling to mount defences and establish a calm stand-off in this surprise encounter.

His mouth curved into a whimsical smile. "We have been introduced."

She summoned up an ironic response. "I remember it well."

His eyes didn't smile. Neither did hers. They appraised each other in a silence that sizzled with undercurrents.

In the days after his brother's death, Annabel had been highly conscious of Daniel Wolfe, reading his reported comments with considerable apprehension and watching him interviewed on television. He didn't raise questions. He posed no problem to her. Yet still she had felt a threat, as she did now.

The camera had reflected the austere elegance of the man, the strong, classically-boned face, the touch of grey at the temples lending a distinguished air to conventionally cut coal-black hair, the tall, broad-shouldered physique clothed in tailored perfection, the aura of control that came with sharply honed intelligence. It had not captured the cold blast of his power to dominate.

Warm charm had been Barry Wolfe's personal trademark.

His brother exuded icy, unshakable command.

A wolf in sheep's clothing tonight, Annabel thought, dismissing the casual image of blue jeans and a dark red sports shirt. The pretence of being on vacation did not wear with her. The laserlike grey eyes were at work trying to strip her of control and strike at any vulnerability he could find.

Her white pants-suit felt flimsy. She needed a steel-plated coat of armour against this man. The soft balminess of the evening suddenly developed a chill. Her arms prickled with goose bumps, despite the long-sleeved overblouse she'd worn in case it was cooler on the walk to her cabin after dinner.

"I much prefer the circumstances of this meeting," he said, as though offering her a truce.

"I was thinking what a small world it is," she replied, the suspicion growing that he had followed her here. Which meant he'd had her under surveillance. For what purpose? was the million-dollar question.

"Growing smaller all the time," he agreed. "Do you mind if I walk with you?"

She shrugged. "Why not?" Better to have him beside her than behind her.

She got her feet working again, and he caught up with her in a few strides. They settled into an easy stroll. The path zigzagged down the hill and was wide enough for there to be no difficulty in avoiding contact. Annabel kept well apart from her unwelcome companion, too intensely aware of him for her comfort. He emanated a more aggressive maleness than she'd met in any other man. It was unnerving, giving the feeling she was threatened on more than one level.

Why did he, of all men, make her feel overly conscious of being a woman? No one could ever have described her as a fragile flower. She was well above average height, with a frame that held generous curves in pleasing proportion and long legs that were strong and athletic from regular gym workouts. His legs, she couldn't help noticing, were longer and stronger, and he was a head taller than she was. Everything about him seemed to put her at a disadvantage.

"Is your sister here, too?"

He asked the question lightly, a seemingly innocuous inquiry. Annabel's inner tension leapt to red alert. Why would he ask about Isabel? To all intents and purposes she and her twin led very separate lives. How did he even know about Isabel?

A bit of probing might be profitable, Annabel decided. She gave him a puzzled look. "Why would you imagine I'd have my sister with me?"

He shrugged. "Twins—identical twins—are very close, aren't they? Perfectly natural to stick together."

There was something very ominous about that knowing little speech. To her perhaps oversensitive mind it suggested he suspected the sister swap. Yet why should he?

"My sister has a husband and three children," Annabel dryly informed him. "We gave up sharing a bed before we went to school."

His mouth twitched in amusement. "I take it you're alone on this trip."

"I happen to like my own company," she said with pointed emphasis.

"Yes," he agreed affably, letting the hint to leave her alone slide right past him. "You come over as unusually self-sufficient. It's quite intriguing, given you're a twin. Are you the older or the younger?"

The harping on twins needled her. "Does age prove anything?"

"I wondered if the stronger was born first."

Annabel had no compunction in tossing the quiz back at him. "Did you find that in your family?" She knew he was the younger brother. Barry Wolfe had been forty-two when he'd died. She remembered reading that the brilliant barrister was six years his junior.

His eyes flashed mocking appreciation for the neat bit of fencing. "If you're comparing me to Barry, it doesn't really apply. We were both first-borns. To different mothers."

Only half-brothers! "Your father was widowed?" she asked, curious about his family situation.

"No. Divorced."

That answered a lot of questions. Barry Wolfe had probably played his divorced parents against each other, learning to double-deal at a very early age and using his considerable charm to get away with it. Whereas Daniel Wolfe undoubtedly grew up enjoying the united focus of both parents. It did make for differences, she decided, apart from those arising from separate genetic pools.

"Were you very close to your half-brother?" she asked, wanting to know his motive for this supposedly accidental encounter with her. Affection? Loyalty? Pride? A wish to clear his family name? Tarnishing hers and Isabel's would not achieve that, but it could muddy the issue and throw doubt on her integrity.

"We were never what you might call close," he answered slowly, "but his company was always lively and interesting when we did get together. Barry was very likable."

His stock in trade, Annabel thought cynically, wishing her sister hadn't been drawn in by it. Although she could understand the attraction, the wicked appeal of a sexy seducer. After eleven years of marriage to Neil Mason—so upright and unimaginative he probably never deviated from the missionary position—Isabel could have been ripe for some creative attention. Annabel inwardly groaned every time she heard Neil pompously declare there was a time and place for everything.

"I shall miss him."

The rueful note in Daniel Wolfe's voice jolted

her. He was human, after all. Not the cold, calculating machine she'd been building him into. It also forced her to realise she shouldn't be judging Barry Wolfe as nothing but a two-faced rat.

There had been many sides to him. Despite his crookedness and lack of conscience about it, he'd been a very popular personality. He'd coloured people's lives. Perhaps that was valued more highly than integrity by people who overlooked anything if they were being entertained by lively company.

"I'm sorry," she said impulsively, then frowned over what seemed an insincerity. She didn't regret Barry Wolfe's death, though she *was* sorry about the loss his brother felt. Family was family, however black the sheep.

She felt Daniel Wolfe's sharp glance at her. Disbelief? Scepticism? She kept her gaze trained ahead, telling herself she was wasting sympathy on him. He was out to get her. Something was niggling him and he wouldn't rest until he had the answers he wanted.

They passed the bridge that led to the administration centre. Annabel thought about checking out of the resort. It wasn't far to Port Douglas. Plenty of facilities there to give her a pleasant vacation. If Daniel Wolfe followed her, she'd know for certain he was pursuing a purpose.

"The last time I saw him was at a fund-raiser for his political party," he said in quiet reminiscence. "Barry was in top form that night, working the crowd for hefty donations. I enjoyed watching him.

He had a knack of making people feel good. Their faces lit up.''

Annabel kept her mouth firmly shut. They'd reached the parking area below the administrative building. She mentally measured the distance to the Long House. Only another five minutes until she could effect a reasonable parting from this troublesome man.

"I saw him talking to your sister."

Alarm bells clanged through her mind. She clenched her teeth. No comment was the safest course. Let him spill out what he knew about Isabel.

"She seemed very taken with him."

Her heart turned over. Had the sexual signals been obvious? Surely Isabel hadn't been too indiscreet, or had she thought herself unobserved? Whatever suspicions Daniel Wolfe harboured, damage control had to be put in place. The need to divert this man's dangerously acute perception, colour it differently, was immediate and critical.

She summoned up a fond smile and said, "Isabel responds warmly to everyone. She's the perfect political wife for Neil. It balances his tendency towards aloofness."

He ruminated over that as they crossed the public road that cut through the resort. Then he startled her by asking, "Have you always been protective of your sister?"

"Whatever made you think that?" she demanded, her eyes wide and innocent.

"Steel and putty."

"I beg your pardon?"

He shook his head at her show of incomprehension. "You're a very smart lady, Annabel Parker. Quite the most tantalising woman I've ever met. So many layers to peel."

"You've lost me."

"No." A ruthless glint in his eyes. "You're with me. Every step of the way."

Annabel had the sense of a trap closing inexorably around her. Rebellion stirred. She stopped in the middle of the parking lot for passing tourists who wanted a drink or a meal in the Long House. There was no incoming or outgoing traffic. She stood stock-still, defying his assertion.

He stopped, too. He turned to her, one eyebrow raised in mocking challenge. "Something wrong?"

"Has anyone ever told you you're insufferably arrogant?"

He grinned. The transformation of his face from hard authority to dazzling magnetism was mesmerising. "Have you noticed how politicians always descend to personal abuse when they don't have a good argument to defend their position?"

It took several seconds for the implication of his words to register. "I wasn't arguing or defending anything. I was stating the literal truth," she insisted tersely, fighting the compelling attraction of eyes sparkling with teasing lights.

"Ah, the truth!" He spoke with relish. "Are you afraid of it, Annabel?"

"No. But I don't necessarily like what people do with it, Mr. Wolfe."

"Call me Daniel. I have a passion for truth. I do hope you share it."

He was dangerous. He could turn on a pin, dodge and weave and strike with devastating cunning and speed. The barrister who could turn black into white.

"I'm not sure I want to share anything with you, Mr Wolfe. I don't know you."

"At this point, you only need to know one thing about me. If one path is blocked, I find another."

He was threatening her with going to Isabel. She sensed the ruthlessness behind the teasing challenge in his eyes. Would he care what he trampled on in going down that path? Isabel's guilty conscience would make her an easy target for him. Then what damage would be done?

"Have dinner with me." He flashed another disarming grin. "It's always better to know the enemy."

Annabel ignored the flutter in her heart and bluntly asked, "Are you my enemy?"

The grin turned into a whimsical smile. "Lovers would be more to my liking."

It took Annabel's breath away. This was no whimsy. He meant it. She could feel it, his desire—will—to peel back every layer of her until nothing was unknown to him.

Well, two could play at that game, she thought with reckless determination. As long as he was engaged with her, he would leave Isabel alone. But becoming lovers? A shiver of apprehension ran down her spine. Daniel Wolfe was not the kind of man who would be satisfied with anything less than everything. All the same, she would give him a hard run to the line he'd drawn, and maybe he'd back off in the end.

"I don't take lovers lightly," she warned.

"Neither do I."

"Dinner I'll accept."

"It's always exciting, embarking on a journey of discovery."

"Yes." Her eyes taunted his confidence. "A pity the reality rarely lives up to the anticipation, but the food is good here. I'm sure we'll find something to enjoy."

With an adrenaline rush at the thought of pitting wits with him over the next couple of hours, Annabel strode ahead, disdaining any fear of him. What was more, she would eat a good dinner even if she choked on every bite. She would not let Daniel Wolfe spoil anything!

CHAPTER FOUR

ANNABEL sipped the pina colada, enjoying the sweet creaminess of the tropical cocktail and the energy lift it gave her. She needed to be sparking on all cylinders in Daniel Wolfe's company. Nevertheless, her primary aim was to appear relaxed and completely unruffled by the situation.

She had deliberately requested a table on the wooden deck by the pool. The atmosphere was more intimate but she preferred to be distanced from the busy comings and goings inside the Long House, where the main dining room catered for a large crowd of guests. The light out here was dimmer, provided only by small table lamps. Her need for a sense of privacy overrode any sense of intimacy Daniel Wolfe might draw from her choice.

With the business of studying menus and making their meal selections over and the waiters gone elsewhere, Annabel let her gaze drift idly around the exotic plants that provided a lush setting for the artistically curved swimming pool. This was Daniel Wolfe's party. It was up to him to set the conversational ball rolling. In projecting the air of pleasing herself, she denied any anxiety or apprehension over his intrusion on the scene.

Silence didn't worry her. The longer it went on the better, as far as she was concerned. She knew he was scrutinising her, trying to burrow under her skin, but that didn't worry her, either. He could study her as much as he liked. With her face in shadow and turned away from him, he wouldn't see much.

"You remind me very strongly of the young Katharine Hepburn," he said bemusedly.

Other people had made the same comment. Annabel supposed she should be flattered by it, since she was not as fine-featured nor as beautiful as the famous actress. It was the wavy red hair, green eyes, high cheekbones and wide mouth that made the comparison inevitable. Secretly she wished simply to be herself. Sometimes, although she deeply loved her sister, being a twin made her feel she wouldn't ever be a whole person in her own right.

She slowly slanted a sardonic smile at Daniel Wolfe. "Do you have the same aim as Spencer Tracy when he first met Katharine Hepburn?"

"What was it?"

"I believe she made a comment about him being too short for her. He reportedly replied he would soon cut her down to size."

He chuckled and shook his head. "It doesn't apply."

"Because you're tall?"

"No. I wouldn't like to see you diminished in any way."

Her eyes mocked him. "What do you think you've been doing?"

It gave him pause for thought.

"Come, Mr. Wolfe. A man with a passion for truth should realise what he's saying and how it will impact on the other person."

"In what way have I offended you?" he asked, genuinely puzzled.

"Diminished, not offended. Let's be precise. In matters of truth, one must be precise."

She enjoyed tossing his purpose in his face, making him examine his attitudes and behaviour before setting himself up as a judge. Besides, there were always so many interpretations of truth. It was often a highly personal thing. Even facts and figures could be twisted to suit someone's preferred vision. Precision was not easily achieved.

He relaxed and smiled, and she thought he was enjoying the mental tussle she was provoking. "Tell me my crime," he encouraged.

He really was extremely attractive when his expression lightened. For one wayward moment, Annabel imagined waking up in the morning with his smiling face on the pillow beside her. It had a strong appeal.

"Let's try this scenario," she invited, leaning forward to engage his concentration. "You take a woman you fancy to bed. There you are, all fired up with desire, and she says you're the spitting image of your brother. Then she says you remind her strongly of Mel Gibson, except your eyes are grey instead of blue. Are you still feeling good about having this woman beside you?"

"No. She's not focused on the person I am."

She grinned at him. "Feeling somewhat diminished, Daniel?"

He gave a wry laugh. "Guilty on two counts," he agreed, conceding the argument to her.

She sat back, ridiculously pleased he had caught her point so quickly. Her eyes flirted with him. She was taking wicked pleasure in putting him on the spot. "I wouldn't like a lover who didn't make me feel uniquely special to him."

Heart-tripping desire flashed out at her. "You are unique. Superficial likenesses are irrelevant to the person you are inside."

She shook her head, trying to quell the treacherous response he evoked as she rebutted his opinion. "They're not really irrelevant, you know. In some ways they shape the inner person." Her mouth twisted ruefully. "Who knows how I would have developed if I hadn't been a twin?"

"The strength of mind and inner fire would still be there," he said with certainty.

"Is that what you see?"

"More like feel. I'd no sooner laid eyes on you than it hit me like a sledgehammer. I've never experienced so much concentrated mental and emotional power. A totally annihilating blast. It made me wonder if you were telepathic."

Had it made him suspicious?

Annabel silently fretted over what might have been a telling overreaction to him that night at the motel. She had been under intense pressure to keep alert and make all the right responses, leaving no crack in her credibility. When he had stepped into the room, she'd been wound up tight, having already fielded a host of questions from the motel people, the ambulance officers, the police. Someone had tipped off the media, as well, and reporters were baying for blood outside.

One look at Daniel Wolfe and all her instincts had screamed, "Danger, threat." Her mind had leapt into overdrive, instantly dictating, "Fight, eliminate." He hadn't said a word, yet she'd repelled him with all the power she could harness because... because she'd felt his power and it had disturbed her, distracted her, and she couldn't afford to be distracted or disturbed. Not until Izzie was safe.

"Are you?" he asked.

The question meant nothing to her. She was still deeply involved in analysing her reaction to him, trying to explain it away. No other man had ever affected her like that. On the other hand, she'd never been in such a nerve-racking, life-and-death situation before.

"You don't want to answer?" he appealed.

"Pardon?"

"Are you telepathic? It's said that twins sometimes are with each other."

She sighed. "There you go again, thinking of me as a twin."

"But not as a carbon copy, Annabel. I would never mistake you for your sister."

Warm pleasure flooded through her as his eyes reinforced his insistence that she was unique to him. Then she remembered the photograph, and her heart seized up. If he had it, could he tell the difference? Most people couldn't with photographs. Her heart kicked into life again. One man's personal opinion didn't count as hard evidence. He'd need more than that to prove it was Isabel who had been with Barry Wolfe when he died.

If that was his intent.

Maybe it was just curiosity to know the truth.

Or was that hope speaking?

The soup was served. Its arrival was very timely. Annabel didn't like the confusion in her mind. She felt a very strong tug of attraction towards Daniel Wolfe. The idea of exploring where they might go together was getting more seductive by the minute. If only their connection had been simple and straightforward. But it was impossible to ignore the complications involved in his identity and hers. She had to stay on guard.

Her mind wandered over the problems as they silently consumed the soup. The truth had to be suppressed. It could hurt too many people. Even if Neil Mason forgave Izzie's lapse into temptation, he wouldn't forget it. His trust in her would be shaken, which would erode the supportive nature of their relationship. This would inevitably rebound on the children, and what had been a happy and secure household would start snapping with tensions.

Izzie wouldn't be able to bear it. She needed approval. She needed someone strong to lean on. That was why she'd married Neil Mason, a man twelve years older and imbued with the confidence of having all the answers to everything, a man who was more than prepared to take charge of his innocent, malleable young wife and direct her along the lines he considered right and proper.

Had Izzie fallen into the marriage because she didn't know what else to do? She had only been twenty. Was it because Annabel had struck out on her own, determined to pursue interests her twin didn't share, tired of suppressing them for Izzie's sake?

Annabel had never voiced these private doubts. Although Neil's pompous righteousness always irritated her, it had felt wrong to criticise a choice when it seemed to fulfil Izzie's needs. However, if she was ruthlessly honest with herself, it had been a relief to pass the responsibility of propping up her sister onto Neil. She had overlooked his faults, wanting Izzie to be happy with him.

But was she?

To go to a motel with Barry Wolfe.

How much guilt did she bear in all this for effecting a separation from her twin to claim a life of her own, knowing Izzie's dependence on continual support?

My other half, Annabel thought with a sense of helplessness. No escape from it. They were two sides of the same coin, different, yet joined to each other in an unbreakable mould that made up the whole. What kind of fate arranged such things? Or was it simply an unfortunate trick of nature? Why, in the split that had taken place to form two of them, was it ordained that one be strong and the other weak?

Steel and putty. Daniel Wolfe's succinct summing up slid into her mind. How had he seen it so quickly? On such brief acquaintance?

Annabel wished it wasn't true. She was always conscious that the division could have gone the other way, with Izzie being the strong one. She knew she could not turn her back on any cry for help from her sister. It wouldn't be right. It wouldn't be fair. It wasn't Izzie's fault that she couldn't cope alone. It wasn't really Annabel's fault, either. It was just how it was.

"It must be a difficult relationship for you, being a twin."

Annabel glanced up sharply, startled at how closely Daniel Wolfe's remark echoed her thoughts. He had finished his soup and was sitting back, watching her. The instant their eyes locked she knew he was satisfied he had guessed right. It gave her an eerie feeling. How had he perceived and understood what she had kept hidden from so many others, even her own family?

Her parents were so proud of their girls, Isabel's marriage, Annabel's career, never really seeing the downside of their duality. Her mother would still be parading them in the same clothes if she had her way, blindly unaware it had made them feel like show dolls, not real people at all.

She looked at her bowl of soup, her hand poised over it with the spoon, and realised she had been brooding over a plate she had emptied, bar a trickle of liquid and a sliver of onion. She couldn't remember tasting what she had eaten.

Troubled at having somehow revealed her secret burden, she carefully set the spoon down and composed herself, deciding to take the initiative from Daniel Wolfe and carry out her own inquisition. His interest in her relationship with her sister was too touchy, better blocked.

When her eyes flicked up again, it was with a look of bland inquiry. "All relationships have their difficulties, don't you think?" Then with barely a pause she attacked, needing to get under his skin. "How do you feel about the pattern of corruption in your half-brother's finance ministry? Does it surprise you?"

His mouth twisted in distaste. "Not really. Barry always had his eye on the main chance."

So he wasn't blind to his half-brother's real character. "Did you know about it before his death?"

"Not in any detailed sense. I had little doubt the rumours were true, but it wasn't my job to look into them, and Barry would never have confessed the truth. He rarely let his left hand know what his right hand was doing. He was a master of manipulation."

The honesty of his assessment surprised her. He was pulling no punches on his half-brother's behalf. Was it possible she could be equally honest with him? Would he be satisfied simply to be told the truth? And let everything lie as it was?

She barely held back the urge to do so. To reach out and... But it was crazy to trust a virtual stranger. Even crazier to confide in any relative of Barry Wolfe's. He might be feeding her lines to see if he hooked something incriminating.

Nevertheless, his comments on his half-brother's character certainly made sense of why her sister had fallen for Barry Wolfe. Izzie was so impressionable she would have been an easy victim for a man who had the knack of discerning other people's needs and weaknesses and had no conscience about playing on them. Annabel nursed a bitter resentment at the callous way her sister had been used.

"He abused trust," she muttered, her eyes flashing her condemnation of such heartless behaviour.

"People whose trust has been abused at an early age tend not to hold much stock in it," Daniel Wolfe answered her evenly. "Trust becomes a commodity to be used in their favour."

"You would have defended him?"

"Everyone has the right to a defence, Annabel."

"Despite how much they hurt others?"

"That's the law. It's always a mistake to rush to judgment. Some people are flawed through no fault of their own. They, too, were once innocent before their circumstances in life twisted them into other paths," he added quietly.

"That doesn't give them the right to do as they please."

"No, it doesn't. Which is why we have prisons."

But his sympathies lay with his half-brother. She didn't like it. She didn't like his legal argument, either, however reasonable it was. There were plenty of people these days who survived their parents' divorces without turning into criminals who took from others when it suited them. To her mind, Barry Wolfe was a crook and a cad.

Daniel Wolfe probably didn't want to hear that. Truth was sometimes very unpalatable. He might try to prove something else. His sense of truth and justice might demand that Izzie pay for falling into the Barry trap, regardless of the circumstances or consequences.

The waiter removed their soup plates.

Annabel picked up her pina colada again. Beyond the lit area around the pool, nightfall was turning the trees into dark silhouettes. She listened for the sound of the surf breaking on the beach, wishing she could recapture the sense of peace she'd felt earlier. It was gone. As was freedom. Daniel Wolfe had to be dealt with, one way or another.

"You're angry," he observed.

She gave him a derisive look. "You revive what I came here to forget for a while. That doesn't exactly please me."

He held her gaze with piercing intensity as he remarked, "One never really escapes from an uneasy conscience."

Annabel laughed, determined to throw him off that line. "My conscience is absolutely clear."

The laser eyes kept boring into her. "Were you personally involved with Barry, Annabel?"

She felt her face hardening and knew her eyes blazed with contempt. "Are you asking me if he was my lover?"

His mouth twisted. "Hormones are not necessarily attached to the brain. Many women found Barry irresistible."

"I found him eminently resistible." She bit out the words emphatically.

"Yet you did meet him at the motel."

"As you so properly pointed out earlier, everyone has the right to a defence." And she would defend Izzie to her last breath. "I was about to kill his career in the public service," she explained for the umpteenth time. "In the interests of fairness, I would grant even a man I despised one last hearing."

"Despise is a strong word."

"You wanted truth. That's it. Like it or lump it, Daniel," she fiercely challenged.

"Such strength of feeling usually denotes that one has been personally hurt. Or—" he paused before adding softly "—someone dear to you has been hurt."

Danger!

Annabel forced herself to calm down, back off. She smiled. Coldly. "Put it down to the passion of a crusader. Barry Wolfe hurt a lot of people. I found his likability offensive. It was a mask of deceit."

"So you weren't ever taken in by him on a personal level?"

She waved dismissively. "He had a reputation as a womaniser. Such men have no appeal to me, however superficially charming they are."

"Then you were armoured against him from the start."

"Armour suggests I might have been vulnerable."

"I've never known Barry to not get a woman he went after."

"That's a sweeping statement. Perhaps he only went after those who showed they were interested."

"And you weren't."

"Not in a million years," she asserted with lofty disdain. "And he knew it. Which was why—" She stopped, appalled at almost tripping into a pitfall.

"Why what?" he prompted.

Why he tried to get at me in other ways. "He didn't like me," she finished with a careless shrug.

"And why he would have enjoyed flirting with your sister, who did like him."

"Did she?" Annabel raised sceptical eyebrows. "Or was she merely returning charm for charm in the superficial way a political wife does at such functions?"

"You would know best," he conceded, but the cynical glint in his eyes telegraphed blatant disbelief in Isabel's innocence.

Annabel felt compelled to cast doubt on his sureness. "You seem biased towards the view that women in general fell like ninepins to the inviting twinkle in Barry Wolfe's baby blue eyes. Did he seduce your women away from you?"

"A few times. It was a game to him. And a useful barometer to me."

"You mean you used him as a test of their interest in you?" The cold-bloodedness of it shocked her.

He laughed. "Hardly that. Barry was older, more sophisticated, more knowing in the ways of women and the world. A flashy sports car, flowers, flattery, fancy places and fun usually won the day. I could have followed his education in this area if I'd wanted to compete with him, but I wanted something different.''

"So he didn't take anyone who really mattered to you," she remarked, secretly glad he wasn't seduced by the superficial.

His thick black lashes swept down, and there was a stillness on his face that gave him a shuttered look. "There was one who mattered," he said quietly.

"What did you do?" she asked, aware she was treading on a sensitive area yet too curious about his reaction—the character of the man—to let it pass.

His smile was chillingly dismissive. "Nothing."

Annabel couldn't believe it. "You just let her go to Barry, knowing him for the philanderer he was?"

He shrugged. "The choice was hers."

"You didn't put up a fight to keep her?"

His eyes flashed with steely pride. "I want a woman who knows her own mind, Annabel. I want a woman who wants me. Exclusively. I'm grateful to Barry for teaching me that.''

Grateful! She shook her head. The hurt behind the lesson must have been dreadful. However much Daniel Wolfe rationalised what his half-brother had done to him, the cruel competitiveness of the game had surely frozen his heart. No wonder he'd perfected icy control, holding back until he could be certain there was to be no shift of interest.

"Is this why you haven't married?" she asked softly.

"Tell me why you haven't," he countered.

"It never felt right for me."

He nodded, emanating a satisfaction that she could feel curling around her. Her stomach clenched as she comprehended what it meant. She'd passed the test of being immune to Barry Wolfe's attractions. He wanted her. Exclusively. He wanted her to want him exclusively.

However much the idea might appeal, it was impossible.

She was a twin.

CHAPTER FIVE

DANIEL found it exciting simply having her walking beside him, climbing the hill together, ostensibly to their cabins. But they were climbing other hills in his mind. Many other hills, with peaks he wanted to reach. With her.

Once she stopped lying.

Didn't she realise it was holding them back? One bold step from her, and they could be past that hump and travelling down the road of truth. He ached for the chance to experience the kind of communication where there were no secrets, no need to suppress anything, no false images. He longed for an honesty that generated mutual trust, where revealing one's true self was not a fear but a joyous freedom, where knowledge of each other was not a weapon but a shared pleasure.

What would it take to pull her over the line she'd drawn in her mind? To make her open up to him? Open in every sense. Daniel felt his loins tighten. She was so infinitely desirable.

The white pants-suit flowed around her, clinging and floating, tantalisingly modest and seductive. Her hair leapt into a froth of flame under every light they passed. In every way she was an enthralling embodiment of fire and ice. He'd never wanted a woman as much. He'd thought what he craved was unattainable, but Annabel Parker held the promise of it. He could feel it...just out of reach.

He played with the idea of catching her hand, imagining the touch of her flesh burning through his. But he didn't want to risk her freezing him off. It was only the first night. He didn't have her measure yet. That, in itself, was exhilarating. A woman who challenged him at every turn.

A woman, moreover, who'd seen straight through Barry.

Daniel grinned. He would like to have seen her in action with his half-brother, that cool, controlled intelligence of hers drilling through Barry's multiple facades and smokescreens, stopping at nothing, refusing to be thrown off track. It was fascinating watching her deal with the problem he was presenting to her—a man who wouldn't be thrown off track.

The private investigator he'd employed to uncover what had really happened with Barry might as well have been on vacation for all he'd achieved. In the past month Annabel Parker had gone about her business with absolute consistency. There had been no meeting with her sister. Her editor verified she had written the article she had cited to the press, although she had subsequently withheld it from publication.

Yet Daniel knew she had lied about that night, and she knew he knew. She was enjoying the sparring. And was incredibly adept at keeping her shield up. Barely a slip tonight, and recovery so swift she left nothing to attack. Very quick to sidestep, as well. Somehow she had to be persuaded to move beyond the duel.

Daniel had always considered himself a civilised man, but her elusiveness was definitely triggering some caveman impulses. The urge to smash down her barriers had to be curbed. He wanted to win her, not drive her away from him.

Not far to their cabins now. They were already starting up the last incline, the steepest leg of the walk, from which they'd diverge onto the path leading to their accommodation. He was extremely conscious of the sexual awareness that had fizzed between them all evening. With any other woman he'd make a move without hesitation. The warning—*I don't take lovers lightly*—held him back.

"What would feel right to you?" he asked, wondering if she had some check list for potential lovers.

She looked askance at him, and he sensed a rise in tension. "Concerning what?" she asked, as though feeling no pressure at all.

Daniel wasn't deceived. The invisible wall around her vibrated with defensive caution. He changed tack to slide in under her guard. "Do you envy your sister's marriage?"

"No. I've never envied Izzie anything," she answered, surprised into a natural response. "Except perhaps her children. They're lovely kids." Green fire flared at him. "Very happy in their home life."

The protective streak again. "Were you happy in your home life as a child?" he tossed back at her.

A slight pause, a whimsical little smile. "Our parents were very loving. Still are."

No mention of the close companionship with her twin. Izzie. It was an affectionate diminutive. Because there had been no meeting with her sister for a month, he'd suspected they'd be coming together up here where they'd feel free to relax and not give rise to the speculation Daniel certainly had in his mind.

He'd been wrong about that, but he doubted he was wrong about anything else. Though it was interesting Annabel didn't like being a twin. No envy—but there was something wrong in that relationship.

"What kind of loving are you looking for?" he asked, wanting more insight into her needs.

She laughed, shooting him a teasing look. "What is this, twenty questions?"

"No." He held her gaze, projecting the intense craving she ignited in him. "Simply a man who'd like to get it right for you."

She halted as though pausing for breath, yet he felt the swirl of turbulent feelings behind the sudden flash of vulnerability in her eyes. Her very stillness was electric, her outer shell in stasis while the powerhouse of her inner energy absorbed his, recording her response to it, playing a roulette wheel of temptation as she weighed the options open to her.

He should have reached for her then, he thought afterwards, but it was as though his body was attacked by pins and needles, a heightened alertness that prickled with an unprecedented sense of anticipation. *Now*, he willed. *Open to me now*!

He felt the door to her mind slam shut almost on the instant. The roulette wheel stopped spinning. The silver ball settled on black. Another spin might bring him the fire he wanted from her, but not tonight.

As quick as the decision was made, she strode ahead of him and skipped up the steps to their private path, turning at the first landing to look at him. "That's not true, Daniel," she said coolly, her chin lifted in proud disdain, her green eyes shooting a clear directive that denied any confusion on this point. "What you'd like is to get it right for *you*."

Bullseye! He couldn't refute it.

She smiled a Mona Lisa smile, slightly taunting, very sure of her own knowledge. "Good night, Daniel."

He found himself caught in a web of admiration and frustration.

She left him behind, a flurry of white heading off to her cabin.

Tomorrow, he thought, mounting the steps to watch her until she was out of sight. There was no glance back. She unlocked her door, stepped inside, and the curtain was firmly lowered on tonight's act with him.

It was only an interval, Daniel assured himself.

Tomorrow they would resume play. She wouldn't be able to leave it alone anymore than he could. There had to be a resolution to all that lay between them. He wouldn't rest content until there was one.

CHAPTER SIX

ANNABEL did not sleep well. Although she had maintained a cool distance between herself and Daniel Wolfe right through dinner and back to her cabin, she couldn't keep him from invading her mind. Her body was staging a mutiny against enforced control, as well, wanting to know how it might feel to be held and kissed by him. Frustrations plagued her at every turn.

Noises in the night didn't help, either. At one point it sounded as though a wild boar was grunting and snorting around outside. A chorus of bird calls woke her at first light, and she gave up trying to sleep. Watching the sun rise from the sea seemed a much better idea. A brisk walk along the beach with a fresh breeze in her face might help clear the fog of fatigue before she had to face Daniel Wolfe again.

He was not about to go away, and trying to escape him would not solve the problem. Somehow she had to steer him off any thought of going to Izzie in his pursuit of truth. He judged women too harshly, especially those who had been drawn in by the charismatic charm of his power-tripping half-brother. No leeway for mistakes or misjudgments in Daniel Wolfe's mind, not where Barry was concerned.

52

The only way out of this predicament, Annabel decided, was to satisfy Daniel with other truths. Achieving this end was not going to be easy. What made it more difficult was having to cope with the tension of resisting him all the time on the personal level. Especially when she didn't really want to.

Nothing was straightforward, she thought despondently as she dragged on her black jeans, donned her favourite lime green T-shirt to cheer herself up and shoved her feet into old black sneakers that could carry her through water and over sharp shells and rocks without being the worse for wear.

Worse for wear she would be if she got deeply involved with Daniel Wolfe. There were so many barriers between them. It simply wasn't worth the emotional turmoil of trying to make choices that would surely come to grief, anyway. She didn't need him in her life. She was fine on her own.

With this conviction firmly in mind, Annabel grabbed her black denim jacket and let herself quietly out of the cabin, wary that her neighbour might also be awake, not wanting to run the risk of alerting him to the fact she was up and about. Time alone was what she needed, time to adjust to the situation and plot a sensible course.

A treacherous rebellion stirred as she passed his cabin. Would it be so stupid to take a chance on his seeing where she was coming from in her life? She liked the way his mind cut straight to the point of everything she said, his ability to listen with an acute focus, his shrewd intelligence. He challenged, he understood quickly, he appreciated her ability to match him in contest, which most men shied away from or resented. Too sharp by half, was the comment usually made about her.

But Daniel Wolfe wasn't put off by it. Approval and pleasure had wafted from him in waves last night. It had been more seductive than anything else he could have done. Physical appeal had never been enough for Annabel. Sympathy, empathy, being tuned to the same wavelength were much more exciting. It was the kind of stimulating togetherness she craved in a partner.

On a couple of regrettable occasions in her twenties she had succumbed to sexual excitement. She'd learnt that passion wore thin when other needs were not met. Each time she had eased out of the relationship, realising it wasn't going to work for either party, not for any long-range intimacy. At thirty-one she was resigned to staying single. She had plenty of friendships to stave off loneliness. And there was always Izzie.

But now there was Daniel....

Maybe today he would do or say something that would be so off-putting, this feeling of wanting to share more with him would pass. In the meantime... She broke into a run, using more concentrated activity to chase away the troublesome treadmill of her thoughts, feet crunching gravel on the tarmac, bouncing echoes off the boardwalk that crossed the gully to the Long House, squishing into the sand on the path from the swimming pool to the beach.

Once past the last line of trees she stopped to

catch her breath and take in the view. Rippling waves shimmered with the light of the rising sun. A boat was steaming along the horizon. Clouds in the sky were tinged with pink and yellow. Birds wheeled overhead and strutted along the water's edge, alert for worms or tiny crabs popping out of the wet sand. Not a single person in sight. She was alone with a bright clean world waking up to a new day. It felt good.

She walked as far as the headland, then sat on a reasonably flat rock to rest, enjoying the solitude, the breeze ruffling her hair, the gentle lapping of the waves and the lovely canvas painted by nature. It was a much calmer sea than she ever saw from a Sydney beach. The high, rolling surf common to the coastline of New South Wales was halted by the Great Barrier Reef in these waters. Annabel was in no danger of being washed off her rock.

Time floated by. Out here it was easy to keep her mind emptied of thought, letting the soft pleasures of the senses drift through. The boat on the horizon disappeared from view. The clouds lost their pretty tints as the sun rose higher. When her stomach started grumbling for breakfast, she glanced along the beach to measure the distance to the Long House and was hit by the sight of Daniel Wolfe strolling towards her.

Although he was still some fifty metres away there was no mistaking who it was, his formidable height, the flash of silver at his temples, the elegant dignity of his bearing—head held high, shoulders straight, long legs moving in the graceful gait of a perfectly coordinated athlete—all stamping him as a man of distinction.

Annabel watched him come to her, monitoring her reaction to him, trying to reason away the sudden quickening of her pulse and the sharpened alertness of tingling anticipation in her mind. Any woman would admire the fine stamp of Daniel Wolfe. A stirring of interest was perfectly natural.

In a more primitive world, he would be at the top of the mating list, prized for his strength and intelligence and the aura of dominating power that would make him a leader of men if he so chose. It puzzled Annabel that he had passively stood by and let Barry Wolfe take women from him. It didn't feel right.

Was he too proud to make a stand for a woman? Did he expect to command her attention by some natural right without having to put any effort into the relationship? If so, he had something to learn about people. In Annabel's experience, there were no perfect fits. Without give and take on both sides, especially the giving, resentments soon set in and undermined the joy of being together.

Yet on her brief acquaintance with Daniel Wolfe, and looking at him now, Annabel found it difficult to see how any woman would prefer Barry. It was the difference between a deep, rich chocolate cake and a stick of fairy floss, one layered with solid substance, the other simply a froth of sugar.

She had the odd sensation of her skin prickling with awareness as he closed in on her, almost as though he projected a magnetic field. Looking away might break it, she thought, but she didn't want to. His eyes gleamed like silver this morning, a captivating contrast to the blackness of his brows and lashes and the olive tone of his skin. He propped a leg on the outcrop of rocks below where she sat and smiled, emitting a warmth that raced through her veins.

"Your hair was like a beacon as I walked along. The sun's rays were bouncing off it as though licking it with fire. It made me wonder if the sirens of the old Greek myths had such fascinating hair."

It was a pleasing compliment. Annabel couldn't help smiling at him. "I wasn't trying to lure you to me."

"I know. You looked entirely wrapped in a world of your own. Am I intruding?"

She shrugged. "I was about to walk back. I'm hungry."

"Have you been here long?"

"Since sunrise."

His gaze dropped briefly to the revealing shadows under her eyes. She hadn't bothered with make-up. A quirky little smile played over his mouth as he gave her a look that shot straight through her defences, jolted her heart and made nonsense of the practical line of logic she had tried to instill in her mind.

"Perhaps we both would have had a more restful night if we'd slept together."

Annabel's breath caught in her throat. Her imagination conjured up a vision of them tangled together, languorously exhausted after the release of all tension, warm, comfortable, content, minds afloat in a pleasurable haze. She barely stopped her gaze from skating down his chest, completing the picture with more physical details. It took considerable willpower to banish the image and force herself to carry on as though his proposition was merely casual banter.

She raised her eyebrows. "Do you often sleep with women on the first night of meeting?"

"I've had a month of nights thinking about you. The desire to experience the reality keeps growing."

"Too fast, Daniel," she stated flatly. "And I can't return the compliment. You were part of a night I didn't like to remember. I associated you with your half-brother. I still do."

He considered the wary reserve in her eyes. "You think I might be a womaniser, too?"

"It seems to me you haven't cared much for the women you've had in your life. You didn't exert yourself to please them as much as your half-brother did."

His eyes hardened to grey slate. "Does a woman need constant flattery to be won?"

Annabel shook her head. "I guess it works on some. I've always felt actions speak louder than words. A woman hardly feels loved and wanted and cherished if her man withdraws to the sidelines as though he doesn't care what she does."

He frowned. "I'm sorry if I inadvertently gave you that impression of me. It's not true."

"You implied you wouldn't compete with your

half-brother. What did you do when he moved in on your women?''

''He didn't do it in front of me, Annabel.'' His mouth curled sardonically. ''And one can hardly compete with a fait accompli.''

So it was done behind Daniel's back. A sneak-thief. She could well imagine Barry Wolfe revelling in stealing from his more upright and highly respected sibling, then parading his victories to demonstrate he was the better man. Such relentless one-upmanship had a vicious and vindictive streak to it.

''He must have hated you, Daniel,'' she said, wondering how any positive feeling towards his half-brother could have been retained.

''Yes. The hatred was there and deep-rooted. I was my father's favourite.'' A wry sadness coated his voice as he added, ''It's wrong for a parent to show preference for one child over another. Barry kicked against it all his life.''

''You're excusing him?''

''I saw a lot of what drove him, Annabel. There was a kind of understanding between us. He knew I knew. I think I was the only one who did. It formed a bond he both hated and needed. Someone who knew him.''

Annabel nodded, accepting the bond of longevity, the mostly unspoken but mutual experience of the inner workings of a family that no outsider really saw or knew.

Daniel heaved a sigh. His eyes darkened as though they were tunnelling back to an empty place in his soul. "I guess we all need that. Someone who knows us."

Yes, she thought, touched, moved by the need he recognised and acknowledged. It was the loneliness of not being known for the person you are deep inside that was the worst loneliness of all. Many people knew bits and pieces, but the totality—not even Izzie comprehended that.

"So you forgave him his trespasses against you," she said, prompting for more.

"There was a time I didn't. I shunned him for years."

"What did he do to you?"

She sensed his reluctance to speak of it. The impression came strongly that he'd locked that part of his life away, not to be touched again. "Truth," he muttered, as though challenging himself to bring it out and lay it in front of her. Then, with a faintly mocking look in his eyes, the tension of decision receded and he spoke.

"Barry took the woman I loved. A week before our wedding. I wanted to kill him."

The one who mattered.

The brief, blunt statements reeked of wildly turbulent passions. Huge hurt. Betrayal. Rage. Shattered faith. Love laid waste.

"They got married," he went on, his voice dry, sieved of all emotion. "It was the only way to justify what they'd done, declaring they'd fallen in love with each other and couldn't help themselves."

Annabel's imagination conjured up the terrible

scene, the power of the man unleashed in fury and pain, even Barry Wolfe quailing before it, suddenly faced with the loss of a man he didn't really want to lose, recognising he had gone too far and hurriedly trying to mend the fence, the woman desperate to defend herself in the eyes of a man whose respect and high regard must have meant something.

"A year later they declared they'd made a mistake and got divorced," Daniel added with a hint of derision.

End of story. But Annabel wondered about the woman. "She must have regretted her choice," she murmured.

"Whether she did or not, some choices are irrevocable," he said flatly. "Nothing could be plainer than that I wasn't the man for her."

A stupid mistake, seduced by an illusion, Annabel thought. Like Izzie. And Neil Mason would feel as deeply cut as Daniel Wolfe had been, even though Izzie had not gone through with it. The thought would be as bad as the act in Neil Mason's black-and-white mind. And Daniel Wolfe might very well share Neil's view on that. No mercy. No second chance. Cast out of his life forever after.

"Why did you let Barry back into your life?" she asked, curious about his attitude towards a man whose sense of rivalry had gone beyond the bounds of tolerance.

"He argued he'd more than paid for his crime, being hung with a wife who'd turned into a hysterical shrew, and he'd done me a big favour in saving me from a fate worse than death, and I ought to be grateful to him.'' He waved a dismissive hand. ''It was the kind of perverse argument Barry excelled in.''

''But you accepted it.''

He shrugged. ''It didn't matter by then. Besides, I'd always known Barry for what he was. I guess the hard blow to take was not knowing Susan as I thought I did.'' An ironic little smile. ''One lives and learns.''

''Yes,'' she agreed, a weight of sadness dragging at her heart.

She couldn't help thinking of lives being changed forever by ill-considered actions, the impulse of a moment sometimes. Did the punishment fit the crime? From seeds sown in haste, there could be a long, bitter harvest. She would do well to keep that in mind with Daniel Wolfe so temptingly on hand.

''I have a compelling urge to know you, Annabel.''

The quiet words punched through her pensive mood. Her stomach contracted. The desire and need to know him in his entirety attacked the caution she had imposed upon herself. She ached to let go all the parameters of her life that confined her, forget everything and live only from this moment, a clean new world, she and Daniel alone in it.

She looked down the beach. Still no one about. The sea a vast stretch of emptiness. Only birds in the sky. They could be on a deserted island. Only the two of them with all the time in the world to know each other, nothing else mattering.

The fantasy shimmered through her mind and winked out. Reality crept back, dampening, dismal, disturbing. She steeled herself to look at him, to deflect the dangerous current of wanting that eroded common sense.

The intensity of purpose radiating from him clutched at her heart. She had to break its pull on her. Action. Diversion. She jumped up from her rock and flashed him a bright smile as she lightly declared, "*I* have a compelling urge to eat." Then she leapt onto the sand and arched him an inquiring look. "Coming?"

"Where you invite, I'll follow," he replied, ruefully amused by her pert tactic to postpone any truth-searching from him.

Follow. The word drummed a warning to Annabel. *Forget the attraction of the man,* she sternly reminded herself, *and concentrate on the danger he represents.* She waited until he fell into step beside her, then raised an issue that had been concerning her since he'd presented himself on her doorstep.

"I didn't invite you to this wilderness resort, Daniel. How did you happen to follow me all the way up here from Sydney?"

"I made a booking straight after you made yours," he answered matter-of-factly.

Coincidence? The same travel agent? She felt there was more to it than that. She took a gamble and asked, "Who tipped you off?"

"I hired a private investigator to report your movements to me."

Despite her suspicion, the ready admission shocked her. Even more so because there was no hint of guilt about it. Annabel frowned. To her it was an underhand, sleazy thing to do. It didn't match Daniel Wolfe's character.

"For how long have you had me spied upon?" she demanded, determined to get at the truth.

"Since the night of Barry's death."

She ground to a halt, more than shocked. Threatened. Frightened. Her mind whirled around the implications of such a decision on his part. If this was because of the photograph... Yet, if he had it, how could he have got it so quickly? What had prompted his investigation? Even if he suspected the sister swap, what did he expect to discover from having her followed?

Or was it personal? Had he been so scarred by his experience with Susan that he had a woman investigated before pursuing an interest in her? Annabel recoiled violently from that idea. The secretive invasion of her privacy for such a purpose bordered on sickness. To have been watched all this time... She shuddered with revulsion.

He had stopped a pace or two from her and was half-turned, watching the play of expressions on her face, making no explanation or apology, just watching.

No desire firing from him now.

All cold calculation.

"Why?" she snapped, hating him in that moment, hating his effect on her.

"I didn't believe you, Annabel," he stated with stark directness.

She stared at him, seeing the relentless drive of the man, and knew he would never give up until he was satisfied he knew the truth. All the truth.

"What..." It was barely a croak. She quickly swallowed and lifted her chin in defiance of anything he thought. "What didn't you believe?" she bit out with scornful precision.

"Your account of what happened that night," he replied, completely unmoved by her stance of high dudgeon, his eyes boring into hers with unwavering conviction.

"What do you suppose happened?" she challenged fiercely.

"I don't know. There is only one thing I know with absolute certainty."

"It must be very comforting to have absolute certainty about anything," she mocked, fighting him with all the strength she could muster.

"I knew Barry for a long time. Your account put him so far out of character it couldn't be believed."

"Please enlighten me."

His mouth tilted with irony. "You're a woman. Barry only ever wanted one thing from a woman. If you'd said you'd gone to the motel to have sex with him I would have believed you. That's not what you said."

"This is ridiculous! His career was at stake."

He shook his head. "You're still a woman. He would never have called you for the purpose you attributed to him, Annabel. He would never have defended himself to you.''

Oh, God! It was true! She knew it the moment he said it. Completely out of character for Barry Wolfe. But she still had to defend her position, protect Izzie.

"Desperate people do desperate things!" she expostulated vehemently.

"Not completely against their grain."

"How can you be so certain?"

"Backed into a corner, Barry would use the same weapons he'd always used."

And he had. Sex with a woman who looked exactly like Annabel, a photograph to prove it, to muddy the waters Annabel had been about to stir.

"With you he had nothing to work on," Daniel went on, hammering home the point. "You didn't like him."

"You only found that out last night," she argued, though it was irrelevant to the thrust of his logic.

"Annabel, whatever went on in that room, my brother ended up dead. I'd like to know—"

"He died of a heart attack," she tersely reminded him. "Natural causes. The autopsy proved that."

"Yes. But it didn't answer the other questions." He paused, letting the weight of her lies hang around her throat before he softly added, "He was family to me, Annabel."

His appeal fell on closed ears. She had family, too, and he was putting them at risk. No way could she tell him what might endanger her sister's security.

Deciding it was best to know the worst, she asked, "So what did your private investigator find out?"

"That you were coming here. And here we both are," he said, and the suggestion of relentless confrontation hung around those words.

Annabel gritted her teeth. She might be running out of space, but she wasn't trapped yet. He could think what he liked. He still had no concrete proof.

She tossed her head, disdaining his certainty. "Well, if you'll excuse me, I need some time to get used to the idea that a man who wants to be my lover has been having me stalked by a private investigator for the past month."

Her eyes flashed contemptuous dismissal as she stepped forward to leave him, well aware she was staging a tactical retreat but feeling perfectly justified in blasting him for his tactics, too. She had not committed any crime. The truth would serve no good purpose. As far as she was concerned, Barry Wolfe was dead, and if Daniel Wolfe wasn't prepared to let him stay dead, he could kiss her goodbye right now.

A hand caught her arm as she passed him.

The knowledge pounded through her—he was not prepared to let anything go.

CHAPTER SEVEN

HE KISSED her.

In a strong whirl of movement that caught Annabel off balance and took her completely by surprise, Daniel Wolfe scooped her into his embrace, plastered her body against his, raked a hand through the thick fall of her hair to hold her head steady and kissed her.

Her mouth had opened to voice a protest. He took advantage of that, too. His storming invasion shattered any coherent thought she might have had, blitzing her mind with a bombardment of sensation. It snapped the control she had clung to, releasing a volatile rush of passion, the pent-up frustrations of her life raging into a need to know all that could be felt with this man, a need to capture every sense of him.

She wasn't aware of her arms winding around his neck, her hands splaying into his hair, her body straining to find the optimum feeling of rightness with his. As their mouths moved in a wildly erotic acceleration of mutual possession, a surge of power arced from one to the other, an electric build-up of intense excitement, an urgency for every kind of contact, a compulsion to explore more and more.

His hand slid under her jacket, tugged at her T-shirt, burrowed under it to spread his direct heat over the bare skin of her back. The shock of her flesh springing alive under the touch of his tripped a recognition of the mad fever that was consuming her. She wanted to experience all of this man, wanted to throw caution to the winds and take for herself, forget the giving, just take and take him into herself until she was someone else, a different entity fused with him, another life.

But it wouldn't happen. In the sane recesses of her mind, she knew it wasn't really possible. A fantasy doomed to disintegrate. With a sob of despair she wrenched her mouth from his and jerked her head aside, gulping in the oxygen needed to clear her brain.

Why him? she railed, torn by a desolate sense of loss in the necessity to reject. Why, of all men, did it have to be Daniel Wolfe who could tap into this deep inner stream of yearning and promise so much in answer to it? It was madness—he was a ruthless man who would stop at nothing to get what he wanted from her. And then condemn her sister.

His lips trailed across her cheek, warmly caressing. His tongue darted around her ear, creating instant havoc. She couldn't bear it. Her hands scrambled to his shoulders, pushing frantically. She shook her head to evade further torment. It had to stop. It had to stop now before she was tempted into an intimacy that could only end in disaster.

"Please…" Her throat was so dry, it came out as a barely audible rasp. She swallowed hard and brought her gaze around to capture his. "This is no good." She forced the words out, her voice shaking with the struggle to reach past the inner chaos of intense arousal.

His eyes were glazed with disbelief, as though he couldn't conceive of her wanting to withdraw from him. They seared her with the accusation of lying as his hand dropped to her buttocks, instinctively pressing a forceful reminder of how their bodies were still reacting to each other, the pliant fitting of her soft femininity around the hard aggression of his fully stirred manhood.

A glittering blaze of conviction dismissed her claim. "Try listening to your body, Annabel. At least it's honest. You can deny it as much as you like, but the wanting is mutual. And that's another thing I now know with absolute certainty."

His insistence sparked a furnace of resentment. "Don't talk of honesty to me, Daniel Wolfe," she flared at him, her hands clenching into fists against his shoulders, ready to beat him away from her if necessary. "You've been thieving from me since day one, and I will not concede anything to a thief."

"I haven't taken anything from you except a kiss. Which you returned in full measure," he fired back at her.

"Having me investigated without my knowledge—it's stealing details of my life you have no right to. Like a peeping Tom," she told him in a fury, feeling helplessly violated.

His chest heaved in a sigh of exasperation. His face tightened, his mouth thinning into a grim line of determination. The challenge to her prejudice came, his eyes powerfully transmitting his will to make her see.

"From the moment I walked into that motel room on the night of Barry's death, you viewed me as the enemy," he stated as irrefutable fact. "I knew you had to be lying, but beyond that puzzle was the intriguing mystery of you, the woman who could look at me and blow me away."

She should do it again. Now! Yet he held her. Not just physically. His mind tugged on hers, swaying her into listening.

"The man I employed provided me with a pattern of your life. Nothing more. I wanted an opening for us to meet on neutral ground. When it came I took it. That's why I'm here, to meet you face-to-face, not to spy. I want honesty between us, and I've given it to you. Why won't you give it to me?"

The appeal, the demand pinned her to a rack of uncertainty. If it were only her life involved... But it wasn't.

"Damn it!" he exploded. "I don't want to fight with you. I want you to share with me. And don't say it's no good. It's too good to let go."

"Then let your brother go, Daniel," she retaliated just as fiercely. "He's dead. And I'm alive. Make your choice!"

He stiffened. She saw his mental recoil and slammed her hands against his chest to push away from him. She burst out of his embrace and backed up a few steps, still facing him, breathing hard, her heart thumping wildly, the determination to throw down the gauntlet to him undaunted by any reaction he might have.

"Not so easy to discard family bonds, is it? That's the truth, Daniel. It's the truth for me, too. I'm not free to give you what you want. Not all of it. Not exclusively. And that's why I say it's no good. I'm being honest."

She turned and blundered away from him, her whole body aching with the burden of unfulfilled needs. Tears pricked her eyes as the deep-rooted desire for a mate who would truly share welled up in her, someone who would complement and complete what was missing in her life, filling the empty places no one had ever filled. It was all so hopeless, hopeless, hopeless.

There was silence behind her. Silence all around her except for the squishing of her sneakers in the sand, the soft slapping of waves, the calls of birds. External sounds. They didn't really impinge on the silence of loneliness.

CHAPTER EIGHT

NOT free!

He didn't believe it.

He'd smashed through her walls, and she was scuttling off to safety, flinging up excuses not to commit herself to what had leapt into passionate life between them. Honesty, be damned! She was afraid of the strength of feeling that had been let loose, appalled that her precious control had been blown to smithereens.

Riven with furious frustration, Daniel wheeled around and strode towards the headland, rejecting her lack of courage as violently as she rejected his invasion of her private world. Which was part sham anyway. She had not been stalked! Her outrage over his use of an investigator sprung from the threat to her deceit. Guilt. Pride. Fear.

And still she clung to the deceit, using the power of his desire for her, giving him an ultimatum—*Let your brother go…*—if he wanted to have any more of her.

No cards on the table from Annabel Parker. She was going to hold onto her hand, and any playing would be on her terms or no deal. Dictating limitations. This much and no more. Cheating what was truly possible. Like Barry.

It was anathema to him.

He reached the rocks where she had sat, where he had spilled his guts to her, wanting her to match him in a pact of trust. He'd opened up to her, and she'd backed away, not willing to risk anything, hugging her apartness as though it was more important to her than what he offered.

It wasn't. God knew he'd been there and done that after Susan let him down, retreating into himself and letting no one close. But there was no contentment in loneliness. It only sharpened needs and made the world more and more an alien place.

He stared broodingly out to sea. The calm water seemed to mock his tumultuous mood. His body ached from the wild fusion of energy she had so wilfully withdrawn from and thrown in his face. He hoped hers ached, too. Every bit as badly as his, since it was her choice to turn it into a bargaining chip.

Let your brother go. He's dead. And I'm alive.

There was a ruthless truth if ever he'd heard one!

The hell of it was he still wanted her. And he'd have her. Why not? She'd handed him the choice of passion with her if he let his passion for truth go. More might come out of it than she planned on giving him. If he walked away he'd be left burning with frustration on every level.

A grim laugh came from his throat. If nothing else, he'd have a sexual experience worth having. At least he'd be satisfied on that score.

Needing to work off some of his deep anger, he hunted among the rocks for some flat stones. Having collected a handful, he stood at the water's edge. Using an old boyhood skill, he threw each stone in a slinging action that set it skipping across the crests of the low waves until its momentum died and it sank.

Like sex, he thought, skimming over the troughs, hitting the highs, then sinking without trace. Annabel Parker was a fool to choose it over what they could have had together, taking the shallows instead of the depths that would have injected it with real lasting power, real substance, endless pleasure.

His last stone skipped six times. It reminded him they were both booked in for six more days at this resort. Six nights. He'd take them and no more, he decided. He was not about to lose his soul to Annabel Parker. He could be every bit as ruthless as she when it came to self-preservation.

CHAPTER NINE

ABOUT a dozen guests were gathered at the far end of the parking area beyond the Round House when Annabel joined the group. It was the departure point for the rainforest familiarisation walk and lecture. She had given it a miss yesterday, wanting to enjoy the bliss of solitude. Today, anything that took her away from Daniel Wolfe and offered distraction was welcome.

They had all been warned upon arrival at the resort that anyone inexperienced with this environment should not wander off alone. Apart from the likelihood of getting lost, there were many dangers to be avoided amongst this most prolific, complex and diverse combination of plants on earth. Not to mention snakes. Australia had more of the deadly variety than any other country in the world.

Every paradise has its serpents, Annabel thought, only half listening to their guide explaining the importance of keeping to the trail. This place would have been the perfect retreat from everything if Daniel Wolfe hadn't come to poison her peace. As it was, she'd felt too agitated and miserable to remain in her cabin. A two-hour stroll in the safety of numbers with the added interest of learning about the rainforest seemed a better option.

The guide was winding up her introductory spiel.

She was quite a pretty woman and very earnest about her job. Her short, honey brown hair was cut in a no-nonsense bob. She wore khaki safari shorts and shirt and very professional walking shoes. Her qualifications were impressive—a university degree in biology plus a research grant for a three-year study of the rainforest frogs, an endangered species close to extinction. She had been at this location long enough to be well acquainted with the area and the trail they were about to take.

"Any questions before we set off?" she asked, her brown eyes flashing brightly around the group.

"Let's go," one of the younger men in the party cut in before any seekers of knowledge could open their mouths. "We can ask questions along the way," he granted as a sop to sensibilities, clearly impatient with information overload and wanting action.

Not such a keen student of nature, Annabel thought, noting his loud clothes and luminous pink baseball cap and wondering if he was going to be the burr in the group. Put a number of people together for any purpose and there always seemed to be one who had to stand out or be difficult, dominating those who preferred to be amiable and easygoing.

When there was no murmur of protest, the guide fell in with his wishes. "Okay, we'll be off then. Oh!" Her gaze darted beyond them and she waved. "Hurry if you're coming. We're about to leave."

One glance and Annabel's heart fluttered and sank.

Daniel Wolfe. Staring straight at her.

He'd been crossing the parking area and stopped when he'd seen her hair. Nothing could be more certain.

Cursing the beacon that had marked her presence in the group, Annabel wrenched her gaze away from him and concentrated her attention on the guide, willing her to get on with her job.

She didn't. She waited, smiling a welcome to the man Annabel most wanted to avoid. He had to be striding towards them, which meant another two hours to bear of his company.

Or she could pull out of the tour.

Retreat again.

Every self-protective instinct screamed to escape from the imminent persecution of his presence, yet a deliberate move away from him now was an admission of fear. She had to maintain the fiction of having no reason to be afraid of him.

Besides, to change her mind about this walk would be letting him have too much power over what decisions she made. She would not openly grant him that. Already this morning she had evaded breakfast in the Long House, picking up some freshly baked muffins on her way through and eating them in her cabin once her stomach had stopped churning from the encounter on the beach. But that was understandable, given his resort to physical—sexual—confrontation.

If only he hadn't kissed her!

She'd been handling the tricky situation fairly well until then, keeping on top of it, fending off the most dangerous points he'd made, casting some doubt on his absolute certainties, she hoped. The kiss had somehow moved all the issues between them onto another plane, and she'd panicked at the intense personal focus that had emerged. Impossible to ignore it or even gloss over it. Which was undoubtedly why she felt so jumpy at Daniel Wolfe's approach.

Yet to leave the group would be so pointed, and it wouldn't resolve anything. Pride insisted she stand firm and find out if she'd had any influence on his thinking. To allow him to rattle her at every turn was counterproductive to maintaining protection for Izzie.

Denying him access to her company was not a wise move, either. He might end up going to her twin, and that had to be avoided at all costs. Faced with Daniel Wolfe, Izzie would self-destruct. So, regardless of her own deep heartburn, Annabel knew she had to face him and keep facing him until he was prepared to go away and stay away.

"Almost missed us," their guide stated cheerily to the newcomer.

"Sorry to keep you."

His voice alone heated Annabel's skin to an acute awareness of his closeness to her. Forget the cocky young man in the baseball cap, she thought derisively. Daniel Wolfe was going to be the burr for her on this tour. And it was impossible to pretend he wasn't there. It would not only be rude, it would indicate how much he disturbed her.

As the guide moved to the head of the group to

lead off along the trail, Annabel shot her nemesis a challenging look, which he caught and held, his laser eyes probing hers with some uncertainty. Had she shaken him out of his seemingly unshakable confidence? It was a seductive thought.

Nevertheless, the need to know more was still driving him. It emanated from him in a wave of purpose that would not be deflected. He sidestepped a couple of people to move in near her for the single-file walk. Annabel mentally girded herself to keep him at arm's length. In every sense.

"Impulse decision?" She lightly tossed the question at him as she set off after the person in front of her.

"No. A choice. Of life over death."

The softly spoken reply had the impact of a missile hitting her right between the shoulder blades. Her spine arched away from it. Her legs wobbled. Her feet somehow kept walking on automatic pilot, but her mind splintered into absolute chaos.

She should have been prepared for his directness. There'd been no real let-up from it since they'd met last night. But this time it really rocked her. She still felt raw from the explosive intimacy that had scraped over her innermost needs, and he was opening up that sensitive area all over again, picking up on her wild demand to make a choice between pursuing the dead past or what he might make of a live future with her.

Or was she misreading what he was saying?

Had he really chosen to dismiss the issues involving his half-brother in favour of having what he could with her? Or was this a trick to get her off guard?

Her nerves were jangling with so much inner turmoil, the tranquillity of the forest didn't even begin to touch her until the person in front stopped to view the fantastic girth and height of a tree being pointed out by the guide. Everyone stopped, their eyes travelling upwards from the huge buttress roots to the canopy of foliage high above them, a fascinating interweaving of branches and leaves with those of all the other towering trees.

The thickness of the canopy completely blocked any sight of the sky, promoting the eerie feeling of being in a vast cavern where the mysteries of growth evolved in fantastic forms—a secretive place beyond the reach of sunshine, permeated by the sense of having existed like this since primeval times, long before man ever walked this earth.

"It makes one feel very insignificant, doesn't it?" Daniel murmured.

"A blink in time," she answered, then looked sharply at him, startled by the harmonious exchange of thoughts.

He smiled, his eyes openly warm, a teasing twinkle inviting a sharing of pleasure. "Togetherness is good," he said softly.

Her heart turned over. "Do you really mean to close the door on Barry's death and what led up to it?" The words fell from her lips, pushed by an urgent need for his assurance.

He nodded. "I know all I need to know."

"You'll let it rest?" she pressed, watching for any hesitation or reservation.

"Yes," he answered unequivocally.

Firm decision was etched on his face. Yet there was a rueful gleam in his eyes, as though her insistence on being free of the issue did not sit entirely well with him. He didn't like restrictions, Annabel thought, and she fiercely wished she could be completely open with him. But trust wasn't earned in a day.

"Move along, you two," the woman behind Daniel said impatiently, alerting them to the fact that the guide was asking everyone to gather close to observe and remember a particular bush to be wary of.

Annabel was acutely conscious of Daniel following on her heels and standing directly behind her shoulder as they positioned themselves for the lecture. He was only centimetres away. His nearness seemed to raise her sensory levels. His body heat was almost tactile, or was it the effect of her skin being warmed by an overactive pulse? She caught the scent of his aftershave lotion. Safari? Definitely an appeal to the wild side. On the other hand, maybe she was simply giddy with relief at being freed from having to fight him.

If he was speaking the truth.

"Whatever you do, don't touch," the guide instructed.

But I want to. I really want to, Annabel thought, remembering how his body had felt, pressed to hers.

"This plant is commonly known as Hairy Mary."

Did Daniel have a hairy chest?

"The leaves are coated with tiny filaments, invisible if you don't look closely. If they brush against your skin you'll know all about it. The sting will be painful and last for hours."

"Makes you wonder about the woman it was named after," the pink baseball cap remarked with a derisive laugh. "Some guy obviously had a hell of an experience."

"Probably deserved it," a woman piped up meaningfully.

It evoked general laughter.

Daniel didn't join in.

Annabel glanced around at him, wondering how scarred he was by the hellish experience of his fiancée's infidelity, virtually on the eve of their wedding. No-one deserved that pain. Had he lost his trust in people? Was that why he had a passion for truth?

His attention was focused on her, and she had the impression he'd been staring at the back of her head, unaware of what was happening with the rest of the group. His gaze flicked to meet hers, and the simmering desire in his eyes made a mush of her mind.

"Your hair smells of lemons," he murmured, and the movement of his lips was seductively sensual.

What would it feel like to have him kissing more than her mouth?

"Come on, you guys!"

They were blocking the path again.

Annabel floated to the next stop in a haze of heightened sexual awareness. She told herself she was crazy to be thinking even half the things she was thinking, but she couldn't help it. She'd never met a man who affected her so strongly.

The group crowded together once more as their guide pointed out a vine to steer clear of. "This is called mother-in-law creeper. See how its thorns are shaped like little hooks? Once it gets those hooks into you…"

"You're a goner," pink baseball cap supplied dolefully.

"Well, not quite. But it can be very difficult and painful to extract oneself."

As it could be from any relationship, Annabel reminded herself. She had no clear vision of any future with Daniel Wolfe. It was more a compelling need to see where they could go together. She had no rosy expectation of marriage or living happily ever after with anyone. It was like a miracle that any man could draw so much feeling from her. That experience itself was more than she had ever anticipated.

But what of him?

If he didn't get entirely what he wanted from her, might he not turn nasty and go to Izzie as a payback for dissatisfaction with the choice she had forced upon him? He might be seeing it as a bargain, and she had no idea what his expectations were… beyond becoming lovers.

"It's rather ironic, bringing the woes of our society into a place like this, isn't it?" he remarked close to her ear.

A frisson of apprehension ran down Annabel's spine. What woes did he have on his mind?

"Naming that vine after a mother-in-law somehow devalues it," he said dryly.

Relief poured through her. Comments on their environment were simple fare for her to deal with. She gazed around at the incredible array of ferns and vines, palms, shrubs, trees, mosses, lichens, fungi, so many species in so many varied shapes.

"Maybe the forest reflects our society," she mused. "Everything here fights for survival in a limited space, adjusting and adapting to claim their bit of territory and hold onto it." She glanced at the man who was making his claim on her. "Aren't we all like that?"

"Perhaps we have an advantage. Instead of fighting, we can make room for each other if we choose to." His eyes bored into hers with compelling intensity. "Will you make room for me?"

"How about making room for us to pass so we can catch up with the others," came a long-suffering voice. "Then you can lag behind as much as you like."

"Sorry," Daniel muttered distractedly, his arm swiftly encompassing Annabel to scoop her against him and draw her out of the way so the frustrated couple behind him could do as they pleased.

The contact with his body ignited a flood of sensation that begged for the freedom to experience everything this man could offer her. Yet caution insisted she feel her way slowly. His tendency to dominate could be too demanding. Once she opened the door to him he might be intent on taking her over, too, and possession in full would never work for her.

"Annabel?" His arm tightened around her waist, pressing for an answer.

She ran her fingernails across the back of his hand. "Always seizing an advantage. I'm not sure I like that, Daniel."

"You're adept at drawing the line. What line is it this time?"

"Room to move. I'll give you space but don't crowd me."

"Fair enough." He loosened his hold.

She spun around to face him. "What do you expect from me?" she asked at point-blank range.

He threw back his head and laughed, a strangely insidious, self-mocking laugh that suggested he expected nothing from anyone. It sobered into a wry smile. "A chance, whatever comes."

"No more than that?" she queried.

His eyes hardened to flint-like cynicism. "Expectations tend to doom one to disappointment, don't you think?"

"Yes. When it stops being mutual wanting, it should stop."

"Let us at least be honest about that."

"You can count on it," she said and swung away, ostensibly to hurry along the trail and join the group but actually wanting to digest all he'd said in the privacy of her own thoughts.

She told herself his attitude suited her, yet it saddened her, as well. And the crack about honesty stung, making her hate the deception she'd felt forced to play out with him for Izzie's sake.

He certainly didn't dream of the happy ever after. Not any more. His Susan had probably put paid to that. And Barry—Wolfe in name and wolf in nature, stealing Daniel's trust, demonstrating a fickleness in female interest that would sour any man's belief in constancy and commitment.

She had the disturbing feeling Daniel had wanted her to be different, wanted her to meet his truth with her truth, matching him every step of the way. She'd failed to do it. And something precious had been lost. The hand he'd initially held out to her had been dropped. This was another option. Better than nothing, but less than it might have been.

The forest suddenly felt oppressive.

She rounded a bend to find the group had moved off the trail and was being herded by the guide towards a pool of sunshine. One of the giant trees of the forest had fallen, tearing a hole in the canopy. The shaft of light from the sky was welcome, breaking the sense of claustrophobia that had started to get to her.

"Now here's the danger," the guide warned as Annabel and Daniel came to halt behind the semicircle of listeners. "It's a natural tendency to head for a break in the canopy, especially if you've been in the forest for a while."

Annabel silently agreed.

"The light is like a beacon to us," the guide went on. "But it's also precisely what the stinging tree likes, and this is where it grows, so always beware of it."

"Well, teach, give us the drum on this monster of the forest," pink baseball cap said cockily.

Annabel rolled her eyes. It was men like him who made the single state look great to women. He also made men like Daniel Wolfe look extra special.

A flicker of vexation crossed the guide's face. She constructed a smile for her star pupil, although her patience with his wisecracks had to be wearing thin. "Men have been known to burn the flesh off their arm rather than endure the agony caused by brushing against these leaves. There's no cure. No antidote. The pain has been known to last for eighteen months, with recurring bouts for years afterwards."

There was a hubbub of horror from the group.

"Again it's the tiny filaments, like fine fur, covering the leaf surface that do the damage," the guide explained.

"The leaves are shaped like hearts," Daniel murmured.

Pain-filled hearts, Annabel thought, and she remembered his words of last night. *I want a woman who knows her own mind. I want a woman who wants me. Exclusively.*

Words born of pain.

Why she suddenly felt driven to make something up to him, she didn't know. She turned to him, and her hand lifted, instinctively placing itself over his heart. Her eyes blazed with absolute clarity of mind as she gave him her truth.

"You're the only man I've ever met whom I really want to know. I have no idea how long that feeling will last, but it's what I feel now."

Surprise, pleasure and a wondering, a weighing flickering through his eyes. Then a slow smile that promised he'd more than meet her desire to know. It set her heart skittering between fear of the unknown and excitement for the adventure.

His hand covered hers, sealing her impulse with the power of a pact. "So we start with that," he said, his voice low, yet the intensity of it winding around her heart, binding her to him.

Annabel had the uneasy sense of having been outmanoeuvred, that his will was done, not hers. Which was ridiculous. It had been her choice. And Daniel had agreed to her terms. She could draw the line wherever and whenever she wanted. The power of decision was hers.

Yet for the rest of their walk through the forest, she could not rid herself of the feeling she was being drawn towards a dangerous place with Daniel Wolfe. Yet it looked so good, the chance to have a really satisfying relationship with a man she felt compatible with in so many ways.

It suddenly came to her that the pool of sunshine had looked good, too, a beacon of light and warmth and comfort, while lurking in the centre of it was the stinging tree.

Was there a stinging tree waiting for her at the end of this journey with Daniel Wolfe?

CHAPTER TEN

ANNABEL glanced at her watch again. Six-ten. Another five minutes before she was to meet Daniel outside his cabin. She took a deep breath to calm fluttering nerves, then laughed at herself. Anyone would think she was a teenager getting ready for her first date, hopelessly indecisive over what to wear, fiddling with costume jewellery, checking and rechecking her make-up, watching the clock.

It was pure female silliness. Daniel Wolfe wouldn't be judging her on her appearance. After all, he had kissed her this morning when she must have been looking her absolute worst. It was something in herself—vanity? some secret wish for the illusion of romance?—pushing her into putting her best face forward tonight. Perhaps all women needed a pretty prelude before plunging into a physical affair.

At least she felt more comfortable about her decision now. The ominous feeling that had plagued her in the forest had been dispelled over lunch in the Long House. Daniel could not have been a more charming companion, adopting the attitude they were here on vacation and interested to know what of the activities offered by the resort would give her the most pleasure.

This had led naturally to a conversation on how

they normally spent their leisure time. Their tastes in books and music were canvassed, other interests touched upon. All in all, the usual exchange between two people wanting to know more about each other, with the heart-lifting experience of discovering they enjoyed many of the same things.

Best of all was the extraordinary and thrilling sense of connection between them, not only physical but mental. That was so rare to Annabel, she couldn't help hugging the excitement of it, couldn't help anticipating how this evening with him would surely end.

Lovers.

Though there didn't have to be any rushing into it. She was sure Daniel would wait until it felt right to her. When fatigue had caught up with her this afternoon, there'd been no protest, no pressure from him to do anything other than her stated intention of collapsing in her cabin for a while. He'd offered to make the bookings for the activities they fancied, showing himself considerate of her wishes and respectful of whatever space she wanted for herself.

She had nothing to worry about, no threat hanging over her head, no conflict bedevilling her. She wanted him, he wanted her, and for the next few days, the rest of the world could look after itself. It was wonderful, marvellous, intoxicating, just to be able to think only of herself and him.

Six-fifteen.

Her heart started hammering as she let herself out of her cabin. Daniel was already on his porch, waiting for her. He looked clean and crisp and vital and virile, his white linen shirt and navy trousers adding dramatic emphasis to his dark good looks and manly physique. His gaze instantly targeted Annabel and remained riveted on her as she walked towards him.

She suddenly didn't care if she was wildly over-dressed. It felt great to make such an impact on him. Besides, she'd always loved wearing this outfit. It was bold and beautiful, the violet silk pants-suit strikingly vivid under a floating overgown that was a glorious patchwork of reds and purples and rich browns and gold. Her Aztec-design copper necklace and earrings added to the exotic effect, which was highlighted by the burnished mass of her red hair rioting above it all.

"I have never seen a more spectacular woman!" Daniel declared.

Annabel laughed and pirouetted in front of him in sheer elation. "Well, since we're off to the Exotic Fruit Tasting in the Loft Bar, I thought I'd get into the spirit of the evening."

He shook his head in stunned appreciation of her vibrant panache. "You could easily have been a megastar in the modelling world. With your height and that gorgeous hair…"

"I did more than enough modelling as a child," she informed him dryly. "I decided very early on I didn't want to spend my life on it." She looked archly at him. "Do you have a thing for models?"

He laughed. "No. I'm fascinated with every facet of you. All of which I hope to explore in depth."

Her stomach quivered. Sexual desire was certainly coming at her, exciting her with its promise, yet the echo of his previous threat—so many layers to peel—rattled her momentarily. Had he really given up his quest for truth where Barry was concerned? Was she being hopelessly neurotic about it?

His eyes seemed to shower her with silvery sparks as he stepped forward and offered his hand, inviting her to accept this link with him for the walk down the hill. It was no more than a friendly, companionable gesture, yet as she submitted to it, she was instantly aware of the power of even this minor physical contact with him.

Her mind pulsed, "Danger."

Her instincts recklessly mutinied against any need for defensive control. They craved the sense of letting go, inviting whatever came, feeling everything that was special about this man.

His fingers deftly interlaced with hers, firming a possessive grip, while his thumb explored the texture of her skin in soft, sensual swirls. Annabel focused intensely on his touch, its tingling effect, the warmth it spread, the curious pleasure of it, the strange comfort and security within the simple sphere of hand-holding.

"What kind of modelling did you do?" he asked as they set off together.

"Oh, just about everything," she answered airily.

Modelling was a long way in the past, no longer relevant to her life. Annabel's mind was fastened on the present. She was thinking his fingers were smooth and supple and very strong, and her pimento nailpolish looked brilliant against the deep tan of his skin, and with him holding her hand as they walked along, the sense of starting out on a journey of discovery was all the more exhilarating.

"Everything? When you were only a child?" Daniel queried, surprised.

His eyes were truly magnetic.

"We started in nappies," she assured him with mock gravity, "and progressed to the catwalk in our teens."

"You mean with your sister?"

It was a natural question. No reason to baulk at it. Izzie was an integral part of her life. It was stupid to read danger into any mention of her.

She smiled, dispelling any darkness as she lightly answered, "Of course. The Titian Twins. We were a big hit. The model agencies loved us. Great gimmick."

"You hated it."

His perception was so swift and sure it evoked a wry admission. "It was like we were always doing what other people wanted us to do. There was very little time to be ourselves. To learn who *we* were."

And Izzie never did learn who she was. A reflection of Annabel, a reflection of their mother and father, her husband, maybe even Barry Wolfe. Daniel was right. Putty. Always pushed by outside forces instead of making and taking a stand of her own. Would she ever be any different?

"Hence the need for your own personal space," Daniel murmured.

Angst twisted through Annabel's soul. Impossible to ever really extricate herself from Izzie's dependency. Her sister's cry of bewilderment still haunted her.

"But what will I do, Anna? They won't want me without you."

"Find something for yourself, Izzie. Something that will make you feel good about being you."

"I feel good doing this."

"I don't."

The irreconcilable conflict.

What supported one twin stifled the other.

"Did your sister feel the same?" Daniel asked, again displaying his eerie ability to tune in on what she was thinking.

"It was a difficult situation," Annabel said evasively, shying away from baldly acknowledging the painful disparity. "Our parents were so proud of us. Even now our family home is like a museum of photographs from all those modelling assignments."

"A lot of parental pressure to keep on doing it?"

"Not really." She struggled to explain the sense of entrapment in a choice made for them before individual choice was even a possibility. "We'd been doing it since we were babies, and the approval factor was so strong, Izzie didn't understand why I wanted to step away from it."

"So you kept on doing it for her sake."

"Mostly. Though Mum was wrapped in it, too. It was an enormous relief to me that Dad came down on my side when I finally opted out. I was feeling so selfish.''

''There's a difference between being selfish and being true to yourself, Annabel,'' Daniel said quietly.

She flashed him a smile lit with pleasure and relief. He understood. The comprehension and sympathy in his eyes were like a soothing balm to the guilt she carried. Impulsively she confided, ''It's not that simple, Daniel. Not when you're a twin. It's hard to separate yourself from the other.''

He nodded. His fingers squeezed hers as though affirming her singularity to him. ''I think your mother has a lot to answer for. She made the sum of you more important than the parts. It must have taken a lot of courage to force the recognition that you were a person in your own right.''

She gave a rueful laugh. ''Am I?''

''Very much so,'' he assured her, his eyes warmly reinforcing her unique specialness to him.

Her heart danced. *I'm not going to think about Izzie any more tonight*, she resolved. *This is for me. All for me.* Five whole days, six nights before she had to go back to Sydney. They could be magic with Daniel. Even short-lived magic was better than none at all.

Amazing how different the mood of this walk was to last night's. So much had changed in a day! Or had it? No, she wasn't going to let doubts in. She was going to fly free. At least for a little while. She deserved it for a little while, didn't she?

Bird calls in the forest, piping clearly in the

lovely stillness of the evening. The air so fresh, like breathing champagne. This special man beside her, holding her hand, promising a togetherness she had never known. The hum of magic all around her, like an exquisite vibration caressing every nerve in her body.

The Long House was a wonderful building, Polynesian in its architectural style though not open to the weather as the great halls Annabel had seen on tropical islands. Nevertheless, the huge, glassed walls at either end gave a similar effect. As she and Daniel entered it tonight, her eyes sparkled over the features that pleased her.

She loved the high ceiling with its massive beams and rafters, supported by specially cut tree trunks. The wooden floor, the cane chairs and the wood tables added to the sense of still being in the midst of nature. The ornamental pool, around which many tables were set, offered the delight of watching a fascinating variety of tropical fish.

The whole place promoted the mood of returning to simple things. Its strong appeal was even stronger this evening. The sense of shedding the complexities of life grew as Annabel preceded Daniel up the staircase to the Loft Bar. The conviction—or was it the wish to believe?—came that it should be as simple as a man and a woman reaching out to each other, drawn by a natural force and responding to it, nothing else getting in the way.

They were greeted by a member of the resort management and handed glasses of champagne. A group of guests had already gathered around the bar for a convivial start to their evening. Neither Annabel nor Daniel was inclined to socialising. By mutual consent they quickly drifted to a corner lounge setting where big squashy cushions softened the cane surfaces and offered sensual comfort. They sank into them and grinned at each other, pleased at having secured a private little nook.

Daniel lifted his glass in a toast. "An evening to remember," he murmured, his eyes telling her she made it so.

The champagne seemed to be bubbling through her blood even before she sipped. Divine madness, she thought, and wondered where the power of the man came from. Physically, he could not be more attractive to her, but that was only the surface. It was the inner drive that fascinated her, tugged on her, too commanding and captivating for her to set aside.

Dangerous, her mind whispered.

A man in a million, her instincts insisted, *worth any risk*.

"What kind of childhood did you have, Daniel?" she asked, curious to know what had shaped the man he'd become.

"Achievement-oriented," he answered wryly. "My father is a work-driven merchant banker, my mother a music teacher who preaches the pursuit of excellence. Ad infinitum."

He rolled his eyes and recited, "Good, better, best, never let it rest, until your good is better and your better best."

Annabel shook her head at the rigid, unrelenting pressure of such teaching, although it did explain how Daniel had reached the top of his profession at a relatively young age. "So you were expected to perform, too," she murmured.

He shrugged. "I enjoyed the challenge, so it was no hardship. But I don't agree with the withdrawal of parental favour if one doesn't meet expectations."

Neither did Annabel. She frowned. "You mean love was measured out according to satisfaction given?"

"It had to be won."

His eyes clouded momentarily. Annabel sensed he was looking inward to a bleak emptiness that craved love that was freely given. Not to have to earn it or fight for it or compete for it. His mouth took on an ironic curl, and his eyes flashed a kind of self-mocking scepticism. Annabel knew intuitively that as much as he might ache for a love that didn't come with a price tag, he no longer believed it was possible.

Even with her.

If you want me, let your brother go.

Again she had the disturbing feeling of something precious having been lost. The desire to make it up to him surged through her heart. Yet she couldn't. The best she could do was not hold out on him any more. Though that was limited, too.

Uncomfortably torn by feelings she couldn't resolve, Annabel seized on the present. She leaned towards him, her smile an open appeal. "Let's not peck over the past. We have *now*, Daniel. We can make the most of now, can't we?"

"Good, better, best?" he teased.

"Why not?"

"I never intended to let it rest, Annabel."

She heard, saw, felt his implacable determination. Panic kicked her stomach. Then he smiled, and the bolt of fear melted away. He meant becoming lovers, not the Barry business.

His eyes definitely said, "Lovers."

The blaze of purpose encompassing her burned with high-octane sexuality, reigniting her passionate desire to live this night to the fullest, savouring every nuance of pleasure in every moment.

As though to stimulate their senses further, a staff member handed them plates with samples of the fruit for tasting. They started, per instruction from their friendly staff lecturer, with the durian and mangosteen, commonly regarded as the king and queen of all tropical fruit.

Daniel declared the durian's flavour surpassed that of any other fruit, but Annabel found it too richly exotic. She much preferred the delicate, sweet-acid segment of mangosteen, its pulp melting deliciously in the mouth.

They watched each other's response to each new tasting experience, enjoying the telling expressions, Annabel's grimace over the too-sweet, fruity brown sugarlike pulp of the sapodilla, Daniel's eye-rolling appreciation of the custard-apple creaminess of the rollinia, their mutual surprise that the rambutans were delectable despite their strange, furry red skin.

It was fun. Most of the fantastic fruits had originated in Central America or southeast Asia and were now grown locally in the tropical climate of far north Queensland, but Annabel had never heard of them, let alone eaten them before, mammee and black sapote, inga bean, and the citrus fruit that tasted just like lemonade without the fizz.

It was more than fun. On a far deeper level than a light exercise in experimentation, other feelings stirred and craved satisfaction.

To Annabel, it was as though she and Daniel had spun off onto another planet, a wildly new and intensely personal experience for them alone. Eating this alien, exotic food was like an initiation, an epicurean adventure to tempt the palate and promise many more blissful rewards for daring to set out, an enticement to journey on, sampling and indulging all the sensual pleasures possible, discovering and sharing them together.

Delicious juices, interesting textures, lingering on their lips, tantalising their tongues, mouths moving in matching action, acutely aware they were tasting the same taste at the same time, the same tingle or creamy satisfaction making the sharing more intimate, more erotic, intensifying the anticipation of their mouths mingling in a deeply sensual kiss, the touch and texture and taste of each other.

Good, better, best.

It was not a poem of pressure but a throbbing beat of need, a compulsive desire to know how true it could be, how far it could go. The exciting sense of rushing towards it promoted a headstrong recklessness, but Annabel didn't care. It had to happen. She wanted it to.

CHAPTER ELEVEN

"WHAT now, Annabel?"

He made her name a caress that feathered down her spine. Beneath half-lowered lashes, his eyes gleamed with the sheen of polished silver, searing her with white-hot sensuality. The softly spoken words marked the end of a silence that had become more and more charged with the anticipation of moving on...taking the next step.

They sat at a table by the pool, the same one they'd occupied the night before. The fruit-tasting in the Loft Bar had finished at eight-thirty. They'd followed it with a light meal, fish, ice-cream, coffee, a glass of fine liqueur port to top it off.

Annabel had been watching Daniel sip his, studying the chiselled contours of his lips, remembering how they'd felt on hers, wanting the same sensational effect again. The sizzling challenge in his eyes, in his words, set her pulse soaring.

"What would you like to do next?" she asked, happy to follow his fancy.

His mouth took on an ironic tilt. "It's your call. I haven't made any secret of what I want with you."

The slightly derisive demand for direction from her jolted Annabel out of her romantic haze. It seemed needlessly crass. Why couldn't they simply be swept along on the seductive mood of the evening, letting it lead wherever it did? It felt wrong to start defining precisely what they were about.

"Aren't my feelings obvious enough?" she queried, not understanding why her desires should be obscure to him. Surely it was impossible for such a perceptive man not to have picked up her signals tonight.

He shrugged. "You could be playing some private power game."

Her recoil from the idea was swift and sharp. "No," she told him, fiercely offended that he should think it.

Yet hadn't she considered using the attraction he felt to subvert any pursuit of Isabel? She'd actually bargained with it, forcing him to put a lid on his passion for truth. Guilt wormed through her. Daniel had good reason to suspect she might be turning the screw further, playing with him, increasing her power to lead him where she wanted him to go.

"No," she repeated emphatically, her eyes blazing with the truth of wanting him for his own sake.

It triggered an answering blaze in his. He leaned forward, reaching across the table to capture her hand and stroke it with strong fingers that dragged at her skin like a set of live wires plugging into the energy within. "I want no holds barred. I want us both naked, hiding nothing. I want to feed on every last drop of passion you possess, Annabel Parker."

The low throb of his voice was like a torch to her inflamed senses. Every nerve, every cell in her body was on fire. Her skin felt almost painfully sensitive, as though it was stretched too tightly, barely holding in the dangerously combustible forces that were racing through her body.

His thumbnail lightly scored the soft flesh in the V of her hand. "If there's a line I'm not to cross, tell me where it is now, before we get up from this table," he commanded.

Her mind jagged out of the mesmerised thrall of imagining herself totally consumed by him. What would she lose? What would she gain? "You're asking for a blanket consent, Daniel?"

"Being called a thief for taking a kiss from you hardly promotes the desire to invite the accusation again."

She stared at him, feeling the pride of the man, the icy control he could and would exert over even the most sizzling passion. *Not tonight*, she thought, her heart drumming with the powerful urge to melt every bit of ice experience had frozen into him. Tonight she wanted the primitive hunter in him released and running free.

"I'm sorry," she said firmly. "That was in the heat of the moment and tied to other issues. It doesn't apply now."

His eyes bored into hers, unrelenting in determining what was in her heart and mind. "You also asked me not to crowd you."

"Why are you trying to pin me down, Daniel? Scared of running risks?" she taunted, pushing for the sense of spontaneity that carried the essence of magic for her.

"I'm not the one who's afraid, Annabel."

The quiet sting caused an instant flare. "Who's asking for guarantees?" she demanded, scorning his caution. "You're the one wanting boundaries to be set. As for being afraid, anyone who has no fear is a fool. But I'm willing to dare with you. Where do you stand, Daniel?"

He grinned, the focused command in his eyes breaking into a prism of sparkling feelings that danced in a wild invitation to dance with him as he withdrew his hand and pushed back his chair to make his stand. "Be bold, sweet maid, and let who will be careful." He tossed the challenge at her.

She rose instantly to her feet to match him. "I believe the quotation is, 'Be good, sweet child, and let who will be clever.'"

He laughed. "I like my version better. My cabin or yours?"

"Mine."

He cocked a teasing eyebrow. "Clinging to control, Annabel?"

"Perhaps I want to smash yours," she retaliated on a wild rush of adrenaline.

"A contest?"

"No." She smiled, revelling in challenging him with his own words. "A journey of discovery."

"Lead the way," he invited with relish, waving his arm in a slow, exaggerated, elegant gesture for her to move ahead of him.

Back to the forest, she thought, and suddenly found herself intensely drawn to the idea of making love in her cabin, surrounded by the dark, brooding fecundity of a rainforest that had been evolving for thousands of years, a wilderness permeated with the mysteries of growth and survival, awesome beauty and danger in waiting.

It wouldn't exactly be man and woman in the Garden of Eden, feeding from the Tree of Knowledge, but close enough, Annabel fancied. The sense of forbidden fruit was there, pulsing through her, the irrevocable step taken into the unknown for the sake of satisfying needs she didn't want to think about. Action was what she craved now.

Up the hill they went, not touching, not speaking, bent on a course that had already been decided upon, the need to fulfil it pulling them on with a power so strong that the apartness and the silence heightened it immeasurably, locking them into a mental and emotional togetherness that found the waiting for its physical expression an exquisite torment, driving anticipation to a peak of passionate wanting.

Her cabin.

Annabel unlocked her door and whirled inside, leaving it wide open for Daniel to follow. The click of its closing seemed unnaturally loud in her ears but every sound seemed magnified, the snap of the light switch, the clatter of her keys on the glass surface of the cane table, the thud of her evening bag landing on the sofa, the pounding of her heart.

She slid her arms out of her coat of many colours and draped it over the back of an armchair as she walked quickly, nervously to the corner of the cabin which could be opened to the outside. She slid the fold-back louvred doors along their tracks, pushing them to concertina at either end of the two-sided screened section, inviting in the tropical night, its scents and sounds, its shadows and its stars.

The overhead light was switched off.

She swung around.

"The trappings of civilisation don't suit us, do they?" Daniel asked, a low, disembodied voice in the darkness.

"No," she whispered.

"Stay there, silhouetted against the sky."

The husky command was strangely seductive. The imagery appealed— The thought of her an outline of solid but mysterious substance rather than the details that made up the whole.

Her eyes adjusted enough to see the pale blur of his white shirt being lifted over his head and tossed aside. Hearing him strip was intensely erotic—the thud of discarded shoes, the slide of a zipper, the shuffle of fabric being removed from his body. It spurred her to rid herself of her own clothing.

A sense of savage freedom gripped her as she discarded garment after garment, imagining his nakedness meeting hers, a collision of raw sexuality, creatures of the night in a mating ritual as old as time. Would his chest be smooth or furred like the wolf he was in name? Would his flesh be hot and hard? What lay under his social veneer?

The coolness of the night air wrapped around her bared skin, raising goose bumps, a weird contrast to the fever raging through her blood. She ran her hands over her body, feeling madly pagan and pumped up.

"A woman standing at the edge of the world," Daniel murmured. "Is that how you feel, Annabel?"

On the brink of something momentous. Yes, but she didn't want to admit it. "No," she said. "I'm standing right on top of it. Care to join me?"

He laughed. It was a ripple of exhilaration, coming towards her as he crossed the dark distance between them, looming like a giant of a man, tall, straight, broad-shouldered, dominant male aggressively primed to claim territory he wanted. His teeth flashed in a wolfish grin as he answered her.

"Actually I'm more in the mood to club you on the head, throw you over my shoulder and carry you off to my cave."

She laughed, exhilarated and exultant that the same primitive impulses were pounding through him. "The club on the head doesn't appeal, but the carrying-off part...are you strong enough?" Her hands skimmed his chest—taut, smooth skin over tightly packed muscle. Tarzan come to life, except Daniel was no apeman. Which made it all the more exciting that he felt this way with her.

His hands gripped her waist and hoisted her high, swinging her around as though showing off booty he'd captured, demonstrating a jungle power she had no hope of matching. But she had female guile and the suppleness of body to wind her legs around his waist and lean back, lifting her hands to ruffle the long, thick mane of her hair into a riotous tumble of abandonment, laughing at the strength that held her, teasing him with what remained free.

"Provocative siren!" he growled, whirling her to the bed where he could kneel over her, pin her down and smother her laughter with a kiss that ravaged and ravished with explosive passion.

It sent shock waves of sensation rolling through Annabel's body. She flung her arms around his neck as her back arched like a bow, taut and thrumming with the electric energy released and running wild. Her breasts grazed the sleek heat of his chest and pressed closer, closer, her heartbeat seeking his to race in unison. His arms burrowed under her, crushing her to him as their mouths invaded with increasing ardour, a fanatical lashing together of forces that drove them into a frenzy of lust for all that could be had.

He suddenly reared away from her, breaking her hold, his eyes glittering at her, his chest heaving as he panted for breath. Annabel didn't mind the pause. She revelled in looking at him, the dark compulsion for possession straining his features, his lips drawn back in a grimace of need, the pulse of his life force pouring through the sinews and tendons of his arms, the sheer virile power of his body poised above hers.

His eyes were drinking her in, too, feasting on the female counterpart of his passion, her soft contours promising pliancy yet allowing him no domination, the whole essence of her being surging in a fiery stream of will and desire to merge with his.

"Yes," she said to him, knowing he was regathering himself and not wanting him to regain any control. In deliberate enticement she lifted her hips to him and scraped her fingernails over the erotic zones under his hipbones.

It drove him wild. He pulled her onto him so fast, the fierce sensation of being deeply shafted by his flesh erupted through her with volcanic force, like hot streams of lava shooting through her body, firing an explosive response. She clawed him to her, claiming his mouth with a passion that fired him into frenzied plunging.

Their bodies boiled around each other, a consuming furnace of mutual possession that strove to reach beyond physical limits, to take it to heights and depths that were buried in their psyches, tapping into their secret selves, opening the closed doors of self-containment and letting go, giving as they'd never given before, falling free, into each other, merging, mingling in an ecstatic, elemental union of spirits that soared and swooped and seized them in a tense, binding rapture, driving them to the unbearable, blissful, ultimate fusion where all energy was spent.

They seemed to implode, bursting inwards with such shattering effect, they collapsed in a limp sprawl, incapable of further movement. Chaos gradually filtering into a deep well of fulfilment, satisfaction, contentment. It was over, what had to happen, yet in completion was the creation of something else. The unknown was now known, and it floated around them, awesome in its released dimensions.

Annabel had no idea how long she lay adrift in a world removed from any reality she had known prior to this night. Her mind feathered around a new imprint of what was possible, shying from fully grasping it.

Then Daniel moved, sliding his arm under her neck, cuddling her close so she lay with her head on his shoulder, and it seemed right and natural.

Fitting together.

Not alone, not apart. Together.

Two hearts beating as one in the live darkness of the primeval forest, throbbing quietly in the stillness of the night.

CHAPTER TWELVE

THEY raced their horses across the sand to the sea. The morning's ride through lowland rainforest and along crystal clear creeks had been delightful but necessarily sedate. It was exhilarating to give their mounts free rein and enjoy the rush of freedom as they headed for the tropical waters off Myall Beach, one of the most beautiful beaches in the world.

Annabel didn't care that Daniel's mare beat hers to the water. He laughed at her mock chagrin, and she laughed, too, hugging the happiness of being with him, loving the way his face lit up with enjoyment, the sparkle in his eyes that said he loved sharing this moment with her, all the moments. There had been a marvellous treasure-house of them in the past three days.

As their horses ploughed into the sea for a swim, Annabel wondered how long heaven could last. It still amazed her that any other person could tune into her mood and thoughts as Daniel did. Sometimes she fantasised that her wish for magic had been answered.

It was as though they'd been bound together in a special spell since becoming lovers. But could the spell extend beyond this place of enchantment? Wasn't it inevitable that it be broken once they left to resume their real lives? Or could they take it with them?

Stupid to let the thought tantalise her. Wiser to simply accept that this was time out of time and be grateful for the experience. Yet it was difficult to banish the tempting vista of it stretching on and on. The more she knew of Daniel Wolfe the more she wanted to keep him in her life.

The water felt ice-cold after the heat of the ride. It reminded Annabel of her first impression of Daniel—icy, unshakable command, and the power to dominate. That was gone now, or relaxed out of existence with the need for it gone. Her eyes gloated over his beautifully muscled back, loving his strength and how he used it to pleasure her.

He turned in his saddle to shoot her an inquisitive look. "It's not like you to lag behind," he teased.

She smiled. "Man, horse, sea, sky...I'm admiring the picture. Very elemental."

His gaze simmered down her body. She'd left a T-shirt on over her swimming costume as her fair skin was quick to burn. The horses had kicked up enough spray to plaster the cotton fabric to her curves, and she was acutely aware of her breasts peaking into the wet cloth in response to Daniel's provocative perusal.

"Your picture is missing a major element—fire," he drawled, his gaze flicking to hers in a look of raw lust. "If we added you to my horse and we were riding together..."

Her stomach flipped. He made everything incredibly sexy. Just a look and she sizzled. A few suggestive words and her mind leapt into a fever of excitement, filling out all the possibilities. It didn't matter what she thought, what she secretly wanted, Daniel always met and surpassed her expectations. Which somehow kept escalating the wild things that flew into her mind. As now...

She saw herself propped in front of him, her thighs in delicious friction with his, her bottom cupped by his loins, the plunging of the horse driving a madly erotic, intimate contact between them. Daniel would have one hand splayed across her stomach to hold her pinioned to him and...

"You could have the reins," he continued, grinning wickedly. "I could bury my face in your hair and ride blind, holding your breasts to keep them warm and protected."

And in a constant state of arousal, Annabel thought, feeling her areolae prickling with sensitivity. She was so distracted by the steamy desires coursing through her that when her horse lurched into a deep trough in the sand bed beneath them, she was dumped into the water. She came up spluttering, pulled along by the reins as her horse began swimming.

Then Daniel was in the water with her, hauling her against him, one arm hugging her around the waist in strong support as he trod water, holding them both above the waves. "You okay?" he asked in quick concern.

She coughed a few times to get her breath back. Silly tears came to her eyes. He could swing so quickly from being fiercely challenging to heart-touchingly tender, Annabel often found herself tossed on a turbulent sea of emotion. She loved both sides of him, yet when he showed his caring for her well-being, it struck some vulnerability in her she wasn't sure she liked. She didn't want to become dependent on his being there for her in so many intimate senses. If... When it ended.

"Annabel?" He turned her gently to face him.

She hung one arm around his neck, swept her hair away from her face and forced a bright smile. "I'm fine. I wasn't paying attention."

"My fault." His eyes danced, applauding her swift recovery. "Want to punish me?"

She laughed. In a sexy mood, he was totally irrepressible. And irresistible. "Why do I feel you'd turn any punishment to your advantage in no time flat?"

"Because—" he kissed her forehead "—you know me—" the tip of her nose "—so well—" her mouth.

It was a salty kiss, an earthy kiss, and quickly grew into a fiery one. "Mmm..." Water was not dampening the growth of Daniel's arousal, either. She gave him an arch look. "I notice you've let your horse go."

"It'll find its own way back to the beach. It's very well-trained."

"I'm not sure my horse is strong enough to carry us both."

"You're right. Better move on to Plan B. Let the reins go. I can walk you in. My feet have found the bottom."

"Feels like your hands have found it, too."

"Mmm...none of the other riders have come out this far. Just hang your arms around my neck and let me rescue you, Annabel."

"I'm really in no danger of drowning, Daniel," she informed him, releasing her horse and following his instructions.

"I think you should be hooked onto me anyway," he replied gravely, moving the lower half of her bikini to one side and gliding himself into a highly erotic position for her to slide onto. "You'll feel much safer like this," he assured her, deftly completing the slick and sensationally sensual link with her.

Annabel leaned back and floated her legs on either side of him, increasing the delicious depth of penetration. "You're right," she said, lowering her eyelashes in a look of sultry satisfaction. "It's such a relief to be rescued."

"Absolutely," he agreed feelingly. "The sexual frustration incited by horse riding can get distinctly uncomfortable. Do you realise it's been at least three hours since I touched you?"

"That long?"

"Mmm..." He rolled up her T-shirt and released her breasts. "Let's pretend these are twin islands in the sea, mountain peaks thrust up from the water. Yes, like that. And I'm a breeze swirling around them..." He bent his head and flicked his tongue around her stiff, protruding nipples. "A tornado," he murmured, and sucked on them.

It was a fantastic feeling, floating weightless in

the water, pleasure arcing sharply from her breasts to the sinfully satisfying union of their lower bodies. Unbelievably, she climaxed with barely any movement at all. Maybe it was getting to be a state of mind, she thought hazily, languorously.

"I think we're being hailed, Daniel," she said, vaguely hearing shouts from the beach.

He lifted his head and sighed. "Well, guess we'd better move in. You could roll around me a bit as I walk."

He raised an arm to signal they were on their way. A few steps later he paused, clutching her bottom as he fiercely spasmed inside her. Then, with an insouciance that set her giggling with the madness of their mutual release, he dragged down her T-shirt, lifted her free of him, adjusted their swimming costumes, and with another cheerful wave to the waiting group, hugged Annabel to his side for the purpose of wading in together.

"Very relaxing swim," he remarked.

"Yes, it took the heat out of us," she agreed.

He chuckled. "I love the way you always have a comeback, Annabel. Have I told you how much I adore your clever mind?"

"No. That's a new one." And immensely pleasing. "So far I've only had glorious hair, a bold spirit, the kind of looks that remind you of Katharine Hepburn..."

"Strike that one. You are definitely one on your own," he strongly asserted.

"A brave heart, great legs, seductive breasts, silky skin," Annabel continued flippantly. "Maybe you should list my parts on a rating scale so I'll know what's most important to you.''

"Impossible. They all make up the magic and mystery of you.''

"Mystery?'' Her eyes laughed at him. "Is there anything left unexplored?''

"At least a million miles still to go,'' he assured her, and behind the twinkle was a glint of purpose that both excited Annabel and gave her a twinge of unease.

It seemed to her they had already travelled light-years from being strangers to lovers, confiding and exploring thoughts and feelings, making personal discoveries that heightened the adventure of being together, increasing the excitement and fun while engendering a harmony that kept strengthening and deepening. How much more did Daniel want?

Neither of them had mentioned any future time beyond this vacation. Was he assuming their involvement would continue past their stay at the resort? Was he beginning to chaff at the limitations imposed at the beginning of it?

She had blocked him from any further exploration of the night of Barry Wolfe's death and Isabel's connection to it. How far could they go together before it came up again? The vista of a very distant horizon shimmered in her mind, so seductive, yet starry-eyed, if she was ruthlessly realistic.

It was impossible to block her twin out of her life. Izzie would be calling her as soon as she went home. Her sister would need another dose of reassurance that everything was all right and any risk of discovery was long past. If Annabel introduced Daniel Wolfe into their world, her twin would see him as a constant and frightening threat to her peace of mind.

It couldn't be done.

Apart from which, Daniel's passion for truth would undoubtedly be triggered again, becoming intrusive, disruptive and ultimately destructive.

He had let the issue of his half-brother lie these past few days, but there had been so much else occupying them, it was easy to put it out of their minds. Besides their highly personal journey of lovers, they'd been very much on the move in other directions.

Yesterday they had taken the boat trip out to the Great Barrier Reef, only thirty minutes away from the resort. The fabulous wonderland of living coral had engrossed them for hours as they went snorkelling, scuba diving, sharing what impressed them most.

The day before that they'd gone on the Noah Valley expedition. Annabel had been particularly interested in the wildlife of the North Range where the rare cassowary bird could still be found. They'd sighted two of them and marvelled over the huge, flightless creatures and their ability to adapt to their habitat.

Today it was horse riding, enlivened immeasurably by other more private activities. Tomorrow they were booked on a chartered trip to Cooktown, and the following day a crocodile cruise on

Cooper's Creek. It didn't matter what they did, it was all extraordinary.

It was not transferable to their real lives.

That was the truth, and it had to be accepted.

By both of them.

Annabel worried over making the position clear to Daniel, then decisively dismissed the idea. It wasn't necessary until it became necessary through force of circumstances. It would be a discordant note in the dream. Why spoil the marvellous sense of harmony?

By the time they reached the beach, their horses were being held by their guide, who urged them to hurry and change into their jeans so they'd be comfortable for the ride back to the stables. Annabel couldn't help smiling over the advice. Daniel had far more original ideas about easing discomfort. Nevertheless, it was nice to climb into dry clothes.

A van was waiting at the stables to transfer them to the resort. It transported Annabel and Daniel right up the hill to the path leading to their cabins, saving them a climb.

"Shower, then lunch?" Daniel suggested.

"Quick shower. I'm ravenous!" Annabel declared.

"If we showered together…"

"No!" She pushed him in the direction of his cabin, laughing at his lecherousness. "We'd never get to lunch. I want food. You've already satisfied my other appetites."

"Damn! The folly of impatience. That was only a brief lifesaver, Annabel. Barely an appetiser."

She skipped away from him. "Save it for dessert."

"Maybe we could try Bombe Alaska?"

"Oh, I expect you to be more creative than that."

Brimming with the anticipation of more adventurous pleasure with Daniel, Annabel didn't see the message slip on the coffee table when she entered her cabin. The shower was her first stop. She quickly stripped off her clothes and stepped under the welcome spray, eager to wash off the sticky feeling of salt and to shampoo her hair, which was a mess after her dumping in the sea.

Having refreshed herself and blown most of the wetness from her hair, Annabel headed straight for her clothes cupboard, not even glancing at the table where the piece of paper awaited her attention. She chose a button-through sundress. More feminine than slacks or jeans, she decided, and Daniel would undoubtedly find the buttons provocative. She left the lower half of them on the skirt undone.

Two and a half days left and three more nights, she thought, determined on living every minute of every hour with Daniel to the full. Such blissful happiness might never come her way again.

Light-headed, light-hearted and light-footed, she twirled over to the lounge where she'd dropped her bag. Her wet costume and towel needed to be hung out before she left to meet Daniel again. In the process of emptying its contents, Annabel turned to lay her purse on the table, and her eye caught the message slip. She snatched it up, a flood of apprehension seizing her mind as she read it.

It was marked urgent.

Caller—Isabel Mason.

Message—Please return the call as soon as possible.

A chill swept through Annabel. The happy world she had embraced stopped spinning. Her heart sank.

It could only mean trouble—bad trouble—for Izzie to call her here in the middle of a well-earned vacation. Something must have blown up about Barry Wolfe. If it was any other problem, their parents were much closer at hand than Annabel to lend whatever assistance was needed. The "urgent" telegraphed fear, and she felt an inability to cope. Yet what was there to be afraid of now, apart from the unstable load of guilt on Izzie's conscience?

Sheer anguish twisted through Annabel. Couldn't Izzie last one week, leave her be for one short week, without calling for help of one kind or another? For one mutinous moment, Annabel crumpled the bitterly intrusive piece of paper in her hand. It wasn't fair. It wasn't right. She had a life, too—with Daniel.

Yet even as she railed against her twin's need, the certainty came that the fear driving the need was real and strong and too solidly based to be ignored. She wrenched herself out of the useless maundering over her lot in life. She had to find out what had gone wrong for Izzie and fix it as best she could, or nothing could be enjoyed, anyway.

Resigned to this incontrovertible fact of life, Annabel grabbed her purse and keys. There was no telephone in her cabin. She had to go to the communications room at reception. Anxious to know the worst as soon as possible, she emerged from her cabin at a run.

It came as a heart-slamming, foot-faltering shock when she saw Daniel casually sitting on the steps of his porch, waiting for her. With Izzie's need billowing large seizing a monopoly on her thoughts, *he* had slipped from her mind. Despite all she had shared with him, felt with him, her love for and loyalty to her twin claimed priority. It always did.

And suddenly she didn't see Daniel as her lover. He was the man who had come seeking the truth—the danger—the embodiment of Izzie's fear—the man who didn't believe Annabel's story of the night Barry Wolfe died.

A convulsive shiver ran down her spine. She sternly cautioned herself. No matter how deeply or strongly Daniel Wolfe tugged on her body and soul, for Izzie's sake, his passion for truth could never, never be fully satisfied!

She'd been sleeping with the enemy, and now she had to slide away from him without awakening any suspicion of trouble related to his half-brother's death and Izzie's connection to it. It was not going to be easy.

Nevertheless, the line was drawn and had to be kept. Daniel could not be allowed to cross it.

CHAPTER THIRTEEN

"SOMETHING wrong?"

Daniel's question was warning enough of how relaxed she had become with him, her thoughts and feelings so quickly and easily picked up. He'd no sooner climbed to his feet from his sprawled position on the porch than he'd perceived something was amiss. His eyes were sharply scanning her expression for other signals.

Her defensive shields felt rusty, but Annabel hauled them into place, reminding herself she couldn't risk letting anyone know what was happening with Izzie, Daniel Wolfe least of all! *Act naturally*, her mind commanded. *Don't let him see you're on guard.* Any abrupt change would alert him to something different having entered the equation of their relationship, and she wasn't ready to deal with that yet. After she called Izzie, then she'd know what had to be done.

She switched on an apologetic smile. "I guess I took longer than you expected. I had to wash my hair." She waved to the steps where he'd been sitting. "You could have come and knocked on my door."

He shook his head. "I didn't want to hassle you. You're entitled to take your time."

Respecting her space.

124

He grinned as he moved to meet her on the path. "Your hair was worth waiting for."

Annabel realised she still held the message slip crumpled in her right hand. Switching it to her other hand would be obvious. Besides, now that any chance of bypassing Daniel was gone, there was no point in hiding it. She pre-empted his taking her hand in his by showing him the piece of paper.

"I had a call while we were out this morning. I should return it before we go to lunch," she said as casually as she could, strolling to get them both moving.

He gave her a sharp glance as he fell into step beside her. "A problem?"

She shrugged. "It shouldn't be. Though I'd like to get it out of the way before we eat. Do you mind?"

"Of course not."

But she could feel the formidable power of his mind clicking through her manner and responses. Did he suspect she was skating over something serious?

Annabel struggled to keep her tension from showing. Daniel was a complication she didn't need in these circumstances. She wanted to concentrate on her twin, get herself mentally prepared to deliver whatever was required.

She walked faster, wishing she could run to reception but holding any hint of panic in tight check. Maybe Izzie simply needed to talk to her. She was prone to working herself into a depression. It didn't have to be disaster looming. Yet even from this far away, Annabel's sixth sense was twitching, warning of trouble. Bad trouble.

"It must be your sister," Daniel said dryly.

Startled, she spoke too sharply. "It's really none of your business who it is, Daniel."

He gave her a sardonic look. "You only shut me out on one subject."

"I don't know what you mean." Stupid lie, but it was out before she could stop it.

Daniel sighed. "Don't insult my intelligence, Annabel. It's a waste of time pretending. I know you too well now."

She flushed, piqued by his certainty. "Pride goes before a fall," she snapped at him.

"It often does," he coolly agreed, his eyes mocking her third attempt at evasion. "Why not run ahead? Get it over with. It's eating you up."

She hesitated, reluctant to admit he was right.

He offered an ironic little smile. "Don't worry. I'll respect your privacy. You can safely make the call without fear of me eavesdropping."

She stared at him a moment longer, thrown into deep turmoil by his all-too-accurate reading of her. It made her feel insecure, as though she'd lost the control to camouflage anything. Somehow he could infiltrate defences that had once been impregnable.

But that was not her immediate and major concern. His disturbing knowingness made caution irrelevant. Pragmatically putting it behind her, she broke into a jog, glad to get away from him and feeling more and more driven to know the worst from Izzie.

It was a relief to find the telephone room at the administration centre empty. She shut the door, hoping no one would enter while she was talking to her twin. At least she was assured Daniel wouldn't. She took the chair farthest from the door and used her telephone card to make the call.

"It's Annabel," she said, the moment the receiver was lifted at the other end of the line.

"How fortuitous!" Neil Mason replied, his pompous words clearly riven with anger. "You have some explaining to do, Annabel. Since I can't get a sensible word out of my wife—"

"Let me talk to Izzie, Neil," Annabel cut in firmly, her hackles rising at his overbearing manner. "In case you don't know it by now, my sister does not respond well to browbeating."

"I notice you don't ask what the problem is," he sniped.

"I'll hear it from Izzie, if you don't mind."

"It so happens I do mind," he shouted at her. "You and my wife have left me open to blackmail with your clandestine carryings-on. And I will not have it, do you hear me?"

Shock rolled through her. It was inescapable disaster if Neil's rantings had any substance! Annabel fought to remain calm, to lift her mind above the emotional blast and inject a voice of cool sanity.

"Yes, I hear you, Neil, though you're not making much sense."

"I will not be swayed from my course." Blind pig-headedness!

Annabel unclenched her jaw and gave some pertinent advice. "You really should practise some flexibility, Neil. Straight lines can cost more than they're worth."

"I am a man of principle," he thundered, clearly not in a listening mood.

"Fine. Then why are you tyrannically taking over my time when I've asked to speak to my sister?"

"She won't speak to me." Furious outrage. "She ran off in a fit of hysterics and locked herself in the bathroom."

Best move she could have made, Annabel thought sardonically. Not that Izzie would have planned it. However, as Neil would say, it was fortuitous. Annabel almost enjoyed reminding her brother-in-law how he had made it fortuitous.

"As I recall, Neil, you installed a telephone in your bathroom to take your important calls while you—"

"Yes, yes," he acknowledged curtly.

"Then just yell through the door and tell Izzie I'm on the line. And a man of principle wouldn't listen in, would he, Neil?"

She couldn't resist pricking his puffed-up self-righteousness, especially when it served the purpose of ensuring a private talk with her distraught twin.

"You think you're so clever, Annabel," he seethed. "I have no doubt you masterminded this deception. But you needn't think I'll be subjected to blackmail to save your face, either."

His receiver crashed down.

Annabel waited, trepidation racing along every

nerve, her heart squeezed tight against the implication that the sister swap had been uncovered by someone bent on perverting Neil Mason's principles. Politics was full of dirty tricks. The question was, did the threat of blackmail have real teeth, or was someone baiting Neil with a lot of hot air and nasty innuendo?

Neil Mason was so staunchly upright he invited being brought down. He could certainly be depended upon to rise to anything. Which did have its advantages. Annabel had no doubt he would inform his wife, albeit with bitter resentment, that her twin was on the telephone. He would have no finger pointed at him for sins of omission or commission.

Locking herself in the bathroom had certainly been Izzie's best move, given Neil's rage. She wasn't capable of withstanding pressure for long. Nevertheless, she couldn't stay in there forever. Her husband did have to be faced. Annabel hoped the situation was retrievable and open to direction.

The click of a receiver being lifted was followed by a wail. "Go away, Neil! At least my sister listens to me." Then came a long, shuddering breath before a plaintive, "Anna, are you there?"

"Yes. Sorry I was out when you rang, Izzie."

"It's hopeless, Anna." Her voice sounded completely washed out, lifeless. "And Neil will make us both pay. I called to warn you and say—" She broke into dry, retching sobs. "I'm sorry...all the trouble...so sorry...my fault."

"Izzie, don't go on, love. Tell me what's wrong."

She blew her nose and tried again. "There's no help this time." Utter despair. "Someone sent Neil the photograph. The one taken outside the door to the motel room. He knows it's me, Anna."

He couldn't, was Annabel's instant reaction. Not for certain. It had to be the power of suggestion. Unless Izzie had cracked and given it away. "How does he know?" she demanded sharply, hoping against hope she had some leeway to work with.

"My rings. It shows my left hand."

It wiped all fight out of Annabel. The incontrovertible evidence. Isabel's engagement and wedding rings. No way could they get around that proof of identity.

"Are they so clear in the photograph?" she asked, desperately casting around for doubt.

"Not in any detail, but it's clear enough there's a ring, and you don't wear any. I do."

Annabel released a long, deflating breath. The game was up, all right. With a vengeance. "What have you told Neil?"

"Nothing. He got the photo in the mail at his office. He came home and accosted me with it. I was so shocked and he was so upset—" Izzie burst into tears again.

"Okay. Worst-case scenario," Annabel muttered. "The trick is to rescue what we can out of it."

"I can't let Neil be blackmailed. Even if he'd do it for my sake..."

Not a chance, Annabel thought grimly.

"It wouldn't ever stop, would it? It'd just go on and on, so it's no use begging him to—"

"I wouldn't suggest it," Annabel cut in decisively, needing to get her sister's thoughts channelled onto the critical problem. "He's spoiling for a showdown, Izzie, and things get said at such times that can't be unsaid later." Control and diplomacy were all-important at this point. "You do have the children to think of, you know."

"Oh, God!" Plummeting despair. "How can I explain meeting Barry? Whatever I say will be an affront to Neil, Anna. He'll never forgive me."

"I can give him another slant on it, Izzie." Best if she drew the fire from Neil. He might be less hard on Izzie if he was convinced she was plotted against, an innocent—well, not exactly innocent, but evilly seduced—pawn in the game. "Can you hold off talking to him until I get there? With any luck, I should be able to catch an evening flight from Cairns."

"You could be here tonight?" A strain of hope.

"Latish, but I'll make it if it's humanly possible, Izzie. At least hold on until you hear from me again. I'll call you as soon as I've made travel arrangements. Okay?"

"Thank you, Anna." Tremulous relief. "I don't know what I'd do without you."

"Well, a burden shared is a burden halved," Annabel returned ironically. She might be able to persuade Neil into thinking twice before ditching his wife and marriage, but her reputation for professional integrity would be shot to pieces once he

made his publish-and-be-damned stand, as he undoubtedly would against a blackmailer.

"You tried to save me from this mess, and now
you're being pulled into it," Izzie moaned regret-
fully.

"My choice. My risk. Don't worry about it.
We'll face it as it comes, Izzie. Try to hold tight
now. I've got to get moving."

She hung up, aware that time was desperately
short if she was to get from Cape Tribulation to
Cairns—a three-hour road trip—in time to catch an
evening flight, if there was a seat available. Then
another three hours in the air before landing in
Sydney. She checked her watch. One thirty-eight.
If she could leave here by two o'clock, and the
connection at Cairns was favourable, she would be
with Izzie at a fairly reasonable hour. If ever her
sister needed full-on support, it was now.

Caught up in the urgency of the situation,
Annabel hurried out of the telephone room only to
be immediately confronted with Daniel Wolfe, who
was casually leaning on the reception counter and
chatting idly with the staff.

He glanced inquiringly at her.

She stopped dead, suddenly drained of her ability
to cope. It was too much for her—Izzie, Daniel,
Barry Wolfe. She wanted to lash out at the fate that
had embroiled her in such a complex tangle. She
wanted to crumple into tears, despite knowing she
could not afford the luxury of such weakness.
She wanted to forget everything and just sink into
her lover's arms and let him sweep her off into a

world of their own where nothing else could touch them.

But that was over, the fantasy she'd indulged herself with.

They were back at the beginning.

With Barry Wolfe.

CHAPTER FOURTEEN

DANIEL silently seethed under his casual demeanour while waiting for Annabel. Everything within him raged against any retreat from the intimacy that had grown between them. It had been so delightfully uninhibited, and not only in a sexual sense. The incredibly deep rapport they'd achieved was everything he'd craved in a relationship. Why couldn't Annabel trust him with the truth now?

No secrets.

There was no need for them.

He didn't want them.

However deeply ingrained this jealously guarded obsession with her twin was, he had to break into it. This conviction was burning through Daniel's mind when the door to the telephone room opened and Annabel stepped out. She saw him and stopped dead.

So did his heart.

She was setting him at a distance, withdrawing, rejecting. He felt his gut tighten. Did the call of her twin have the power to obliterate everything they'd shared?

His mind switched to battle stations. He was going to fight like hell to keep doors open between them. If he had to smash them down, he would. It was totally irrational of Annabel to block him out

134

now. Surely she realised he was not blind to Isabel's claim on her life. There was no need for this clutching it all to herself.

She moved stiffly to the desk as though reluctant to come close to him, forcing herself to do what had to be done. Ignoring his presence, she addressed the receptionist in a crisp, clear tone that was mind-controlled, inadvertently revealing intense inner turmoil.

"I have to be in Sydney tonight. It's a family emergency. Can you arrange the necessary transport for me?"

"The normal transfer bus has already gone, Miss Parker. I can probably charter a safari vehicle but the cost will be—"

"What about chartering a helicopter?" Daniel broke in.

They gave him startled looks.

"Can it be done or not?" he pressed.

"I can try," the receptionist answered.

"Daniel." Annabel swallowed. She looked sick. Her green eyes had no fire in them. She seemed drained of the energy he associated with her. "This isn't your affair," she stated flatly.

Everything to do with her was his affair. He'd had a taste of what their life could be like together, and nothing was going to stop him from pursuing it. Ruthless and relentless determination welled up in him, though he clamped enough control on it to keep his voice light and reasonable.

"There's no point in my staying here alone, Annabel. I'll fly back to Sydney with you." He turned to the receptionist. "Work on making the fastest arrangements to connect with a flight from Cairns to Sydney. Cost no object. Book it to me."

"Yes, Mr. Wolfe."

He targeted the other receptionist. "We haven't eaten. Ring the restaurant to make up a picnic lunch for us. Have them bring it here. In the meantime, get our accounts ready to be settled. We'll go and pack. We'll need a resort van to collect our luggage from our cabins."

"Yes, Mr. Wolfe."

"Daniel…" Annabel was working up to protest his interference again.

"It's an emergency, right?"

"Yes, but…" Anguish in her eyes.

"I can see you're shaken up, Annabel. Just ride with me, and I'll get you home as soon as possible." He swept the receptionists a commanding look. "I'm trusting you to really move on this. Do the best you can."

"Yes, sir!" they chorused.

"Let's go." He hooked his arm around Annabel's waist and scooped her along with him. "I'll make you a coffee in your cabin."

She sighed in surrender and pushed her legs into action. "A helicopter will cost a fortune," she muttered. "I can't let you pay for it."

"Fine. We'll go halves. You can take the next fifty years to pay off your half to me if it's a problem."

She spun out of his hold, her eyes flashing a painful warning. "Don't tie yourself to me, Daniel.

What we've had up here…it's not going to carry over. It can't.''

"I'll take my chances on that."

She gave a negative jerk of her head. The decision not to argue was written clearly on her face as she turned and strode along the boardwalk to the track up the hill. He was right behind her, determined to follow wherever she went. He was not about to let her cut him off as though he was no more than a vacation lover whose services and company were no longer required.

"I take it Isabel needs you," he said, attacking the protective wall she'd built around her twin.

"Yes." She trudged on in silence, obviously not prepared to amplify her shut-out reply.

"Why?" he asked.

Her face was white and strained. "You said you would defend your half-brother, that everyone had the right to a defence."

"Your sister needs you to defend her?" he swiftly interpreted. "Who's accusing her? Of what?"

"You said you understood Barry," she went on, ignoring his questions, hammering out her internal argument. "Longevity. Familiarity. You were the only one who really knew him."

"I imagine it must be much more so with a twin," he said, tuning in on where she was going.

Her eyes were touchingly vulnerable as she flashed him a grateful look for his understanding. "I have to be there for her, Daniel. I think that, left alone, Izzie would destroy herself."

"The dependency is that strong?"

"It'll be worse now. I won't have time for you. Not the kind of time you'd want." A flat statement of fact, reality as she saw it. She looked at him with bleak resignation. "It would tear us apart anyway. Two's company. Three's a crowd."

"She has a husband, Annabel," he pointed out.

Her mouth twisted in bitter irony. "Probably not, after today."

Neil Mason shedding his wife? Daniel's mind leapt to adultery, to Barry, to what he'd suspected all along, to the conclusion he'd come to.

"How did Mason find out about Barry?"

The question was logical to him, but it startled Annabel. She stopped and stared at him, her expression oddly blank as though her life was passing before her eyes. Her mouth moved into a rueful little smile. "Well, I guess I can at least answer your passion for truth, Daniel. There's no point to my holding it from you any more."

"I'd appreciate your telling me," he said quietly, sympathetic to her sense of defeat while inwardly elated at her surrender to his persistence.

She plodded up the track, moving because she had to. "Barry knew I was working on an exposé. His only way to get at me was through my sister." She shook her head in a private remonstrance at her own blindness. "I had no idea Izzie was in contact with him, let alone susceptible."

"He intended to use her to stop you?"

"One bell was as good as another," she quoted. "That's what he told Izzie when she started arguing with him at the motel. He'd had a photographer snap them as they entered the room. It frightened her. She wanted to leave."

"It was a set-up?"

"Yes. But he didn't like her saying no at the last minute. He got a bit rough with her."

"He would have been pumped up, pulling off such a scheme," Daniel acknowledged.

She paused for a breath and cast him a challenging look, ready to strike at any show of disbelief from him. "Izzie fought him off. He suddenly collapsed on her."

He nodded sympathetically.

"She did her best to revive him with mouth-to-mouth resuscitation. She'd done a St. John's Ambulance course, Daniel, so she wasn't unskilled."

The defence against any accusation of negligence in not calling for help immediately. It was reasonable, and he accepted it, though it was unnecessary in the circumstances.

"I'm impressed that she stayed to help him," Daniel reassured her. "I know it wasn't her fault he died, Annabel. The autopsy showed a massive heart attack. There was nothing anyone could have done to save him."

The fire in her eyes faded. She heaved a sigh as though a burden was lifted. "Well, he was certainly dead when she rang me. Fifteen or twenty minutes had gone by. Izzie was in a blind panic. The photograph could prove she'd been there."

"Or you'd been there."

She nodded. "It's almost impossible to tell us apart in photos."

"So you took her place and toughed it out."

"If Izzie had stayed, the scandal would have blown her marriage apart. Barry wouldn't have targeted her but for me, Daniel." There was a strained appeal in her voice as she added, "I know you'll say she had a choice, but you don't know her as I do."

His mind flitted to Susan, the choice between Barry and himself. But it wasn't the same. Isabel had said no. It might have taken the shock of being photographed to break the excitement of seduction and bring her face to face with the sobering reality of what she was risking, but she had backed off from the final betrayal. She had chosen her husband and children, although too late to save herself from being dragged through so much mud it would undoubtedly stick in Neil Mason's craw and make it too unpalatable for him to swallow.

"You're right. She was more a victim than a sinner," he conceded. "I understand your rushing in to protect her, Annabel."

A wry little smile seemed to dismiss his understanding, as though it no longer mattered. She turned her gaze tiredly up the hill and pushed on. "It's all about to crash in on us now," she said dully.

He frowned as he caught up with her. How could the cover-up unravel? It had been so rock-tight he had been unable to crack it. "Has Isabel broken down and confessed?"

"No. And I'm hoping she can hold on until I get there, or Neil is likely to throw the baby out with the bathwater, and Izzie will just drown in it all. I don't know how yet, but I might be able to contain the damage."

"What does she have to hold on against?"

It earned a sardonic look. "Neil's bull-at-a-gate cross-examination. Someone sent him the photograph. It's some kind of attempt at blackmail."

"But isn't the photo inconclusive for identification purposes?"

"It shows Izzie's left hand. Her rings. Neil is demanding an explanation." She shot him a derisive look. "What price the truth, Daniel? Does it sit well with you now you've got it?"

"Yes, it does," he said quietly. "Like the last pieces of a jigsaw being set into place. It gives me satisfaction."

She gave a bitter laugh. "Well, it'll probably give a lot of other people satisfaction to see Izzie and me publicly crucified. Neil has a passion for truth, too."

"Surely he's not so stupid as to go public with this."

"He will not be blackmailed." Her voice was harsh, contemptuously dismissive of any soft thinking. "What do you imagine that means, Daniel? Following your belief that people always act in character."

The challenge served to sharpen his brain again. "You'll be sacrificed to his principles," he answered unequivocally, realising that Neil Mason's ego was entrenched in his black-and-white preachings.

"Tossed to the wolves." Her eyes mocked the pun. "Your half-brother wins from the grave."

No, Daniel thought fiercely. Barry was not going to reach out from the grave and take this woman from him. He was convinced he would never meet her like again, and he'd fight tooth and nail to keep what they'd found together.

They reached her cabin. She unlocked the door and swung to face him, her back rigid, her shoulders straight, her eyes coldly resolute. "It's better if we break now, Daniel. It'll be cleaner for both of us."

"Let me help, Annabel," he demanded more than appealed.

"Look, I'm grateful for your quick sense of organisation, but—"

"Precisely. I'll take care of the travel details while you concentrate on what you have to do for your sister. Now let's get on with it. I'll make us some coffee while you start your packing."

She looked mutinous for a moment, then accepted his usefulness without further argument, shrugging off his persistence with a terse comment, "Don't say I didn't tell you the truth."

He was well aware she could be as ruthless as he in her decisions. It was her enormous strength of mind that had first attracted and excited him, though he had since come to believe she was the sexiest woman on earth, not to mention other fascinating attributes that constantly held him in thrall.

He stepped into the bathroom where the coffee things were kept. What he needed most was a solution to the crisis that had arisen. Annabel had spelled out the consequences she and her sister were facing as a result of the incriminating photograph, and Daniel could not fault her judgment. If the photo was accepted... But did it have to be? It all hinged on the rings. If Isabel kept her mouth shut...

He shook his head over the wild plan that leapt to mind. Any kind of deception was anathema to him, yet what if the only way to fight lies was with lies? Hadn't Annabel faced the very same decision? And acted to protect good against evil, seeing that as the ultimate goal?

Be damned if he would let Barry win!

The electric kettle whistled. He poured the boiling water over the coffee granules, added sugar, then carried the cups to the living room. The clothes cupboard stood empty. The suitcase on the bed was already full. Annabel was roving the room, picking up belongings. Daniel set the cups on the table, took a deep breath and moved to intercept her path to the suitcase.

She frowned impatiently at him. "Don't get in my way, Daniel."

"Stop and listen to me, Annabel. There's a way out of this mess if you're willing to take it."

It won her attention, but her eyes were sceptical. "You can show me a path I haven't seen?"

"You know what Isabel's rings look like?"

"Of course."

"Describe them."

"Her engagement ring is an emerald with baguette diamonds on either side. The wedding ring is a simple gold band."

"Right! Here is the scenario. You and I became engaged before that night with Barry. I'd given you a similar ring to Isabel's but with a wider band. You were wearing it. That should cover whatever's in the photograph."

She stared at him in stunned disbelief. "You're prepared to lie?"

"Sometimes fiction can serve justice better than truth," he declared, mentally balancing the scales, aware that all too often the punishment meted out by the media didn't fit the crime. In this instance, he could see nothing good being served by the truth. Apart from which, his future was at stake!

She shook her head dazedly. "It's crazy anyway. You and I hadn't even met before that night. We were actually introduced…"

"The blackmailer won't know what's gone on in our private lives, Annabel. We can be very convincing about what we feel for each other now. I have no problem with standing by you and declaring it in public."

She looked away distractedly as though he'd introduced an element she couldn't quite comprehend. Did a trusting partnership with him feel so foreign to her? If he'd misjudged… No, damn it! He couldn't be wrong. Their involvement with each other on every level was too mutual to be mistaken.

He slid his hands around her upper arms, lightly

grasping to focus her attention on him. Her eyes were anxious, panicky, shying from meeting his.

"It can work, Annabel," he asserted firmly. "It's all perfectly reasonable. We broke up because of a misunderstanding over that night. You were furious with me for not trusting you, and gave me back the ring. That's why you haven't been wearing it all this time."

"It's more lies, Daniel," she cried, twisting in the wind of forces she couldn't control.

"It could have been true, given a slight time shift," he said persuasively. "My interest in you dates from that night. I followed you up here to woo you again. You've agreed to become re-engaged to me."

"What about the ring?"

"I have it at home. I can get one made in Sydney tomorrow so we can produce it as proof."

She stared at him, torn between hope and anguished uncertainty. "Do you realise you'd be tying yourself to this fabrication? You'd have to pretend to be my fiancé."

"I have no difficulty with that."

"I can't even guess how far you might have to take it."

"I'm happy to take it as far as it goes." He lifted his hand and stroked her cheek reassuringly. "Trust me. I can carry it off."

He grinned a devil-may-care grin to lift her spirits, stepped over to the table, picked up her cup of coffee and pressed it into her hand. "Think about it while I go and pack. Together we'll make a formidable team against anyone.''

Daniel left quickly, wanting Annabel to think it through herself. He was a distraction to the real nub of this affair—her twin, whom she wanted to save. His plan would establish Isabel Mason as Caesar's wife—beyond reproach. If tying herself to a partnership with him achieved that end, Annabel would choose it. Consistency in character. Daniel was banking on it.

It was a partnership that ensured a place for him in her life. An intimate place. One that could not be set aside at will.

Truth and lies...the means to an end.

Maybe Barry was winning, after all.

Daniel didn't care at this point.

He was still in the game.

CHAPTER FIFTEEN

THE five-forty flight from Cairns to Sydney landed precisely on time. Because Daniel had organised first-class seats for them, their bags headed the file of luggage on the carousel. They were in a taxi and on their way to Brighton-Le-Sands before nine o'clock. The last leg of the journey.

But a journey to where? Annabel worried, acutely conscious of Daniel sitting beside her, taking a place in her life that she hadn't counted on anywhere along the line. She wasn't used to relying on anyone else for anything that was personally important to her. She'd never done it, never had any need to. She found it unsettling. The closer they got to Izzie's home, the more uneasy she felt about accepting his proposition.

Not that she doubted his word or his ability to act on it. He would do and say whatever was necessary to block the scandals that would erupt if the sister swap was revealed. His power to dominate would emerge—as it had at the resort this afternoon—and people would automatically fall in with his command. It was not a question of trust or confidence in him that was troubling her.

It just felt strange having him beside her, knowing she was about to depend on him in resolving a close family matter, letting him into a private world of knowledge that had always been hers alone.

Reason argued she needed him to help save the day. Which was fine in principle, absolutely logical and practical, yet Annabel suddenly realised it was the need that was needling her. It took away her choices. She didn't have the freedom to change her mind. She had to depend on him. Needing Daniel to stand with her was an entirely different thing to wanting him there.

She did want him.

She didn't like needing him.

It felt like a trap.

"Why are you doing this for me?" The words shot out of her mouth. She looked sharply at Daniel, who appeared perfectly relaxed, sitting quietly beside her in the back seat of the taxi.

His eyes met hers He weighed the question, seeing its importance to her. "Many reasons. But essentially?"

"Yes, essentially," she urged, too wound up to mince words.

"Because I don't want what we shared up there to stop," he said, giving her the directness she had come to value, the honesty that had generated an intimacy she had never known before. He reached out and took her hand, lacing his fingers through hers. "I like our togetherness, Annabel. It feels good."

Yes, it did. Her heart fluttered with positive appreciation. Warmth from his hand soothed her jangling nerves. She had thought their togetherness couldn't be translated to their real lives, but maybe it could. Her eyes locked with his, and it was like an infusion of energy, a flow of wild and mutual certainty that together they were more, apart they were less.

Kiss me, she thought.

He leaned over, cupped her face and filled her mouth with the powerful magic of his. Her blood sang. She didn't want what they shared to stop, either. Her hand slid around his neck, holding on, feeling how good it was not to be alone.

The taxi slowed to a halt.

The next step, Annabel thought, and was glad Daniel was with her, taking some of the load off her shoulders. Neil would automatically respect him, a barrister of his stature, a man of law. Izzie... God only knew what Izzie would think!

For Annabel to have any man in tow at a family crisis would completely throw her. The fact that Daniel was Barry Wolfe's half-brother would send her into a spin. But she would survive. That was the point to hammer home. With Daniel supporting them, her marriage and family could survive intact. And Annabel's professional reputation would not be tarnished.

Surely Izzie would welcome the means to that end, though the nature of it would be disturbing to her. It meant having to accept that her ever-dependable twin was attached to someone else. But Izzie had Neil, Annabel fiercely argued to herself. Why shouldn't she have Daniel? He understood what had to be done for Izzie. No one else had ever understood her as he did, so quickly and comprehensively she hardly had to explain anything.

She took a few deep breaths to lower her tension as they paid off the taxi and carried their luggage to the house. At least the children would be in bed at this hour. Izzie would have used caring for them to fend off Neil's pursuit of an explanation that would satisfy him, but it would have been sheer torture for her. The past hour would have been the worst. Annabel rang the doorbell, hoping it signalled relief to her sister.

Predictably, Neil opened the door, determined on ruling the roost over both twins. He was a big bull of a man, broad-shouldered and barrel-chested and very short-necked. His head seemed to sit aggressively on his big, muscly shoulders, and he projected a look of dominant power. Bully power, Annabel always thought, but Neil was certainly an impressive man, quite strikingly handsome with his crinkly blond hair and bright blue eyes. He could be genial and charming when he wasn't being authoritarian, but authority was on show tonight.

He was taken aback to see Daniel with Annabel, his mouth opening and closing as he thought better of the greeting he'd had on his tongue. Daniel was taller than Neil and his physique was hardly what one might call weedy. More to the point, he surpassed Neil in exuding authority, the icy command of the man projecting a silent but very real natural dominance.

Neil was even more taken aback when the formidable figure beside his sister-in-law was introduced. The name Daniel Wolfe carried clout on many levels in this situation. Circumspection was in order. Although Neil suffered tunnel vision in his idea of what was right and wrong, he was far from being a fool. With prudent dignity, he ushered his visitors into the living room, where Izzie had apparently been ordered to wait.

She sat nervously on the front edge of an armchair, her fingers fretting in her lap, her eyes huge pools of anguish as she looked at Annabel, then swirling with wild confusion at the unexpected introduction of Daniel. She stood to greet him, desperately trying to project grace under pressure.

Annabel moved swiftly to give her a reassuring hug and the automatic support of simply being together. "It's all right," she whispered. "He's on our side."

"He knows?" Shock was swiftly followed by horror at Annabel's betrayal of what had been their secret. "How could you? You made me promise not to tell Neil."

"Daniel can help us and make it stick, Izzie."

"But…"

"Hush now. I'll tell you in a minute." Annabel swung around to face the men, curling her arm around her twin's waist at the same time. "Izzie and I will get us some coffee while you and Daniel are getting acquainted, Neil." She smiled cajolingly. "It has been a long trip from Cape Tribulation."

Neil glared his disapproval of this arrangement, but politeness held sway, and he was inviting

Daniel to make himself comfortable as Annabel swept her twin out to the kitchen.

"What are you doing with him?" Izzie cried in agitation the moment they were beyond earshot.

Annabel calmly told her the rescue plan while carrying through the stated purpose of making coffee. Her twin did not take the news at all calmly.

"How could you take Daniel Wolfe as your lover?" Half-shrieked as though it was the crime of the century.

"He's everything I ever wanted in a man," Annabel said truthfully, wanting her twin to realise and appreciate how special Daniel was.

"You're shameless, Anna." Sparks of righteous reproof. "Using your body to get him to do what you want."

Annabel rolled her eyes. Her twin was beginning to sound as priggish as Neil, never mind that *she* had started this mess by fancying Barry Wolfe as a lover.

"It's not like that," she corrected with some asperity. "I happen to find Daniel very sympathetic and extremely attractive."

"So was Barry Wolfe, and he *used* me. How do you know Daniel Wolfe isn't using you?"

"Because it isn't just a sexual affair, Izzie. It goes much deeper than the physical. Believe me. I know Daniel is committed to doing what he can for us."

It rattled her sister. "But you're not really going to marry him."

"It hardly matters if I do or not. The point is—"

"I know what the point is. Another lie." Izzie's voice rose on a hysterical note. "Involving a man in *my* life who's a stranger to *me*."

"You could try trusting my judgment, Izzie. I've done a damned good job of protecting you so far," Annabel said tersely, impatient with irrelevant objections.

"He's not family. He's not even related to us. And you're using him against Neil."

"*Against* him?" The accusation rankled. Exasperated by her sister's lack of clear vision, Annabel fired a fog-lifting blast. "It's to *save* you and Neil from getting yourselves in a stupid twist where both of you lose what you've got. Now do you want to be saved or not?"

"Not by your very convenient lover," came the fiercely resentful retort. "You've got no right to bring in someone you go to bed with and set him up to fool my husband. I thought you'd have more loyalty than that, Anna."

"Loyalty! For God's sake!" Annabel couldn't believe what she was hearing. She exploded with a few home truths. "I've laid myself on the line for you, Isabel. As for making a fool of Neil, it was you who did that by going with Barry Wolfe in the first place. I've put myself through hell to save you from the consequences of your own folly, and you challenge *my* loyalty? What about yours to me?"

Izzie burst into tears. "I can't bear it. I just can't bear it."

"You'll bear all the muckraking a whole lot less," Annabel stated bluntly. She grabbed her twin's shoulders and tried to shake some sense into her. "Pull yourself together, Izzie. We can ride through this."

The reaction was almost violently negative. Isabel started working herself into a manic frenzy. "You've got that man now. You won't want me. You're letting him take over."

Jealousy? Possessiveness? Annabel shook her head in bewilderment and quickly denied the charge. "No, I'm not."

"You're doing what you want. You always do what you want." Bitter resentment.

"That's not true," Annabel defended heatedly. "This is for you. And Neil."

"You've got no right to interfere with us." She pulled away, flapping her hands to ward off Annabel as though she was a plague. "You should leave us alone."

"Now hang on a moment. You called me for help. I broke off my vacation, flew thousands of kilometres—"

"I didn't call Daniel Wolfe for help."

The selfish unfairness of her sister's attitude riled Annabel into sizzling vehemence. "Well, it so happens I want his help, Izzie. You're not the only one involved in this."

"I didn't ask you to get involved."

"You called. You accepted everything I offered."

"You made me think it was right. But it's not right. And I'm not going to listen to you any more." Her eyes stabbed savage, irrational hatred

at Annabel. "You and Daniel Wolfe bypassing me
as though I was nothing. I'll do it my way."

She whirled off down the hallway, leaving
Annabel too stunned to make any move to stop her.
There was no logic to any of this, Annabel thought
dazedly, trying to sort her way through the erratic,
emotional storm rained on her by her twin. The attack simply wasn't justified on any level of reason.
Izzie had to be out of her mind.

Having reached this conclusion, Annabel hurried
after her, anxious over what her twin would do next
and how much damaging fallout there would be
from doing it her way. Whatever that meant. Con-
fession might be good for the soul, but throwing
herself on Neil's mercy would be like handing him
a brick to beat her with.

She arrived in the living room to find Isabel already taking action. Daniel had apparently asked
Neil to show him the photograph. He was seated in
an armchair, Neil hovering beside him. Their attention had obviously been fastened on the photo in
Daniel's hands until Isabel refocused it, confronting
both of them in a brave show of facing up to the
situation, tears shimmering in her eyes, voice tremulous.

"I don't know what he's been telling you, Neil,
but I won't keep the truth from you any longer. It
is me in this photograph." She snatched it out of
Daniel's hands and started tearing it up in a frenzy
of rejection and disgust as she sobbed. "It was a
trick, a terrible lie to ruin us if Annabel didn't do
what Barry Wolfe wanted."

Annabel froze in the doorway. It was her twin's scene, and there was nothing she could do about it now. Daniel leaned back in his chair, a look of fascinated interest on his face as he observed Isabel's act for her husband. Neil's expression wavered between affront and belligerence.

Isabel plunged on, wailing an appeal for understanding. "You were out at a meeting that night, Neil, so I couldn't ask you what to do. The children were staying over at Mother's, and I was all alone when the call came from Barry Wolfe."

"Why would he call you, Isabel?" Neil demanded aggressively, clearly upset at having been kept in the dark for so long.

"He said Anna wanted me to come and help her," she cried, letting the last bits of the photograph fall out of her grasp so her hands could be used to express her dilemma. "He said she was having some kind of attack and could hardly breathe. I thought it must be the asthma she used to get."

"You should have told him to take her to a hospital or call an ambulance," Neil said brusquely, his eyebrows beetling disapproval, his ruddy skin blotching with a build-up of inner heat.

"You're so right, Neil. If only I'd done that…" Wringing of hands. Despair. An anguished twist of the head as she continued. "That dreadful man said Anna didn't want anyone to know they were meeting. It was at a motel. He said she insisted I could help. She knows I keep Ventolin handy for when David gets his attacks."

Annabel stared incredulously at her sister. She was weaving her son into the story, touching on a sympathetic chord, knowing how much Neil worried over the boy's asthma.

"If only you'd been here..." Izzie wrung her hands even more eloquently, her eyes brimming as she begged her husband's forgiveness for her impulsive actions. "I could only think Anna was in trouble. She's my twin, Neil. I felt I had to go. She was asking for my help. At least, I believed she was."

Neil glared at Annabel, only too ready to see her as the scapegoat for any sins his wife might have. "You're too easily swayed, Isabel," he bit out, but it was obvious where he was beginning to place blame. He'd always been jealous of the close relationship between the sisters, resenting what he saw as Annabel's influence on his wife.

"It was so awful, Neil," Isabel cried, clasping her hands over her heart. "When I got to the motel, Barry Wolfe was waiting in the car park, and he hustled me straight to the room where Annabel was supposed to be. We were just outside the door when that photograph was taken. The flashlight startled me. Before I knew it, he'd rushed me inside. And Anna wasn't there." The shock in her voice carried dramatic impact.

"The lying bastard," Neil growled, completely taken in.

"He said he was going to keep me there to prove I was having an affair with him and then he'd blackmail Annabel into not printing the truth about his dirty dealings. I was so frightened, Neil." A fountain of tears.

Neil was moved to fold her into a comforting embrace. Isabel clung to him, a pathetic picture of wounded innocence, crying her heart out.

Annabel, staggered by the artful performance of her twin, who had always seemed so helpless, tottered over to the closest armchair and sank into it, feeling as though scales were being ripped from her eyes. She needed at least the comfort of a secure chair under her.

Daniel shot her a look of caring concern, but she motioned him to remain still and silent. *Let the play run its course*, she thought, feeling a bitter sense of betrayal and wanting to gauge the extent of her twin's duplicity in her dealings with all of them, however disillusioning it proved to be. Annabel had a passion for truth, too.

"I tried to get away," her sister sobbed into Neil's expansive chest. "I was fighting him when he collapsed and…and I thought it was my fault. I didn't want him to die, Neil, even though he was a bad man. And I'd learnt mouth-to-mouth resuscitation for the children. Especially for David. I did all I could to revive him." She choked on more tears.

"It was very brave of you," Neil soothed, patting her back in comfort and approval.

"Then when I couldn't get him to breathe again… Oh, God! I didn't know what to do." She snuffled into Neil's chest, soaking it for more support. "I couldn't just leave a—a dead man like he was nothing. I rang home but you weren't there. Then I remembered the photograph and worried what everyone would think. So I rang Anna and she—she…''

''Took over,'' Neil finished for her, his eyes like swords of retribution, stabbing at Annabel.

''She told me to go home and forget it,'' Izzie went on in a heartbreaking wail. ''What happened wasn't my fault, Neil. Anna knew straightaway it was a trick to get at her, so she said she'd handle everything. And if the photo showed up no-one would know it wasn't her. I thought—I thought she was right, and I was so frightened.…''

''You did wrong to keep it from me, Isabel,'' Neil said sternly, but the accusation was really levelled at Annabel, his eyes pinned inexorably on her.

''I wanted to tell you, Neil. It's been so awful having to keep it to myself. But Anna made me promise.''

''Liars will always be found out,'' Neil declared, the wrath of God in his voice.

Isabel shuddered and lifted a wet, piteous face. ''Anna said the media would turn my being at the motel with Barry Wolfe into something dirty and smear our marriage. I kept silent for you, Neil. It wasn't fair if they hurt you. You're so good.…'' More heart-rending sobs.

''There, there, my love,'' Neil said gruffly. ''I know your heart is in the right place.''

Saint Isabel, all her sins washed away.

''You've been badly misled by your sister.''

Evil Annabel, immured in the wicked ways of the world.

"But virtue will triumph. I promise you. So don't you worry your pretty head any more. I'll take care of everything for you. I'll set that fellow straight tomorrow. I'll sue him for all he's worth if he prints anything questionable about my wife."

The shining white knight, lance lowered, ready to charge on behalf of his fair maiden.

Annabel felt sick. She had to clench her teeth against the rush of bile up her throat, then swallowed hard to get rid of it. *Used*, she thought. *Used and abused.*

Daniel turned his gaze from the newly reunited couple and gave her a long, searching look. *Are you going to let this be?* he seemed to ask. She couldn't summon the energy to think about it. Her mind registered what was happening, but she was totally lost on what to do, or if, indeed, there was anything to be done. She shook her head, finding no will to act at all, giving up the ground to whomever wanted to take it.

Daniel did. She saw resolution march onto his face. His laser-like eyes turned from her to Neil. He was going to enter the fray and challenge the white knight, Annabel thought. Which should be interesting to watch. She'd never had a man fight for her honour. She was glad Daniel was prepared to do it. It proved how special he was.

CHAPTER SIXTEEN

"PARDON me the intrusion on this reconciliation with your wife, Neil," Daniel stated gravely, "but you did mention blackmail to Annabel."

It was as good a bombshell as any to throw into the ring at this point. Pertinent, as well. Annabel was amazed she had forgotten it. Which said something about the state of her mind.

Isabel's face turned from Neil's sopping wet shirt, her suddenly dry eyes shooting a drop-dead look at Daniel, who comprehensively ignored her, concentrating his attention solely on the white knight. Neil frowned, unsure of Daniel's position.

"As Annabel's legal representative," Daniel enlightened him portentously, "I'd like to know about the fellow you intend to straighten out tomorrow. You haven't told us where the photograph came from or what use of it is being threatened." He paused and threw in the weight of law. "Annabel certainly has a right to know."

It was a clever tactic, lifting the issue out of the personal realm and into legal process. Annabel silently applauded it from the sideline. She felt too drained to bother with anything herself, drained and disgusted and so deeply divided from her twin it was akin to facing a death.

"It came from a journalist," Neil replied pettishly, feeling at a disadvantage against Daniel's expert knowledge. "It was clear to me he wanted to run some gutter story featuring my wife and Barry Wolfe. These journalists are all the same." Another glare at Annabel, working himself up to outrage again. "They'll do anything for a sensational scoop."

"You must have the journalist's name," Daniel prompted.

"Jack Mitchell. He works for a rival newspaper," Neil added, directing the information at Annabel as though that was her fault, too.

"I know Jack Mitchell," Daniel said quietly. "He did me the kindness of telling me the circumstances of Barry's death before the rest of the media jumped on the bandwagon. I've always found him to be a reporter of considerable integrity. You may have mistaken his intentions, Neil."

It brought forth a belligerent frown. "The man sent me the photo and said if I didn't comment he'd draw his own conclusions. He gave me until tomorrow to consider my position."

It wasn't blackmail, after all, Annabel thought wearily, simply the proper procedure for a journalist of any integrity, checking the source before running with a story. She knew Jack Mitchell professionally. He would have checked with her, too, if she had been available.

"I believe it would be in the interests of all parties if the story was killed," Daniel stated in a very formal tone. "I'd appreciate it, Neil, if you'd leave that in my hands."

It stung Neil's pride. "I have nothing to fear," he declared pompously.

"There is certainly nothing against you in it," Daniel agreed. "However, in consideration to your wife, who might be harassed by the press, and your sister-in-law, who acted to protect your wife's good reputation, I feel discretion is the better part of valour in this instance."

"I'm more than prepared to stand by my wife," Neil blustered. "As for Annabel, she brought this upon herself, and—"

"No, she didn't," Daniel interrupted forcefully. "Barry set this up to get himself out of trouble and I consider it a grave injustice that Annabel should pay for his wrongdoing."

"Two wrongs don't make a right," Neil pompously preached.

"A stand on that issue could be made on something much more worthy than the circumstances of my brother's death," Daniel pointed out. "I might add that the truth as we now know it—"

Brilliantly rearranged to serve the self-interests of her twin, Annabel thought bleakly.

"—would add to the pain my family has been suffering," Daniel said with an emphasis designed to draw sympathy. "The scandals about Barry's dealings have hit them very hard." He paused before softly appealing to Neil. "Is it needful to you that they be hit once again?"

The plea for mercy got to Neil. He was not a vindictive man. Certainly not with innocent people.

"It would be a kindness to my parents, who have

been deeply shamed, through no fault of their own, if you let me handle Jack Mitchell, Neil,'' Daniel pressed. ''There are a few points of law I'd like to draw to his attention. If he insists on going ahead with the story, I'll have him contact you for your statement, but I hope he will see the sense of letting it die. After all, it serves no good purpose.''

The ultimate persuader. Daniel did read people extremely well. The emphasis on the words ''no good purpose'' appealed to the high moral ground Neil liked to occupy.

He's won, Annabel thought even before Neil signalled surrender. Part of her mind said she should feel pleased and proud of her man, but no feelings came. It was as though she was removed from the whole scene, watching it from a distance, like an out-of-body experience.

She couldn't bring herself to care what was decided. Isabel had cut it out of her, the caring. It was lying on the floor, discarded like an old shoe that no longer fitted, its value used up, not worth keeping.

Neil stared at Daniel for several long, tense moments. Perhaps the relentless purpose of the man was dawning on him. Whatever the reason, he gave up the fight and assented to Daniel's course of action.

''Very well. I'll leave it in your hands. But I would be obliged if you let me know the outcome.''

Isabel's lips thinned. She didn't like Neil being bested by Daniel, but there was nothing she could do about it if she wanted to retain her mantle of virtue. Strange how she expected Annabel to keep silent about her flirtation with Barry Wolfe, yet she had made no move to persuade Neil to accept Daniel's offer to kill the story. She either didn't care how Annabel would be affected—or actually wanted her wounded.

"Thank you. I appreciate your confidence," Daniel said graciously. "Now, if I may use your telephone to call a taxi…" He rose to his feet, tall, formidable, commanding.

"Yes. Neil and I would like to be on our own now," Isabel rushed out plaintively. "I daresay you'll take Anna home." A cursory glance at her twin. "She must be very tired."

"Be assured I will look after your sister, Isabel. And watch out for her interests," Daniel said quietly.

The underlying tone of threat should have chilled Isabel to the bone. It certainly made her jump. "I'll make the call for you. We always get taxis very quickly here, being close to the airport. Shouldn't be more than five minutes," she gabbled on her way to the door.

Neil watched her go, his bullish face softened to an expression of benevolent indulgence. "This has been very traumatic for my wife," he explained to Daniel. "She's not as strong as Annabel."

"People have different strengths," Daniel answered diplomatically.

"Absolutely. Isabel is the perfect wife for me. And a wonderful mother. Very strong in that regard."

"You're a lucky man."

"Yes. My wife has all the right instincts. I'm afraid Annabel has a tendency to guide her by her own lights, and that is completely wrong for Isabel." A frown for the bad twin.

"I have no doubt Annabel appreciates that now, Neil," Daniel said with a touch of dry irony. "Let's remember that what was done was done from the best of all possible motives, and it has been a very difficult time for her, too, without anyone else adding to it at this point."

"It never pays to deceive," Neil growled.

Annabel reflected that her twin had her fooled all their lives. She suspected Isabel was perfectly capable of pulling the wool over Neil's eyes for as long as she wanted. In fact, as a manipulator, Isabel was beginning to look like a good match for Barry Wolfe. If he hadn't died, there might have been an entirely different story eventuating from that night.

Impossible now to assume that anything Isabel had told her was true. It had served her purpose of getting out of a hot spot scot-free. And landing Annabel right in it. Which suddenly had very familiar echoes down through the years.

"I've been out of touch with all the local news," Daniel said, bluntly ignoring Neil's pious homily. "Far North Queensland is like another country. What's been happening here?"

It filled in time.

Annabel was not interested in current news items.

Her memory started sliding out old themes—patterns of guilt, compensation, fixing things for Izzie, taking blame, taking responsibility, doing things she didn't want to do, like the modelling, because it was easier than bearing her twin's traumatic tears and worries. A lot of power in weeping and wailing, Annabel thought with newborn cynicism.

It was almost laughable, thinking of herself as the strong one. Looking back now, she saw herself as a puppet being pulled by strings manipulated artfully by her twin under the guise of helplessness. Her rebellion against modelling and her insistence on going to business college were the only strong stands she had made against the insidious tentacles of Izzie's needs.

How early had the behavioural pattern been set? Her parents laughingly recounted how Annabel had walked at nine months old and Isabel hadn't managed it until twice that age, but it didn't worry Izzie because she only had to point to something and cry for Annabel to fetch it for her. Like Pavlov's dog. Automatic response.

No more, Annabel resolved. The puppet would not dance to Izzie's tune ever again. Her twin could start taking responsibility for her own decisions and actions. The fall guy was retiring and could not be recalled.

A horn beeped outside.

Izzie appeared in the doorway. "That's the taxi now," she announced, eager to see them out of her domain.

"I'll help carry your bags out," Neil offered, very chummy now all was settled to his satisfaction.

"Good of you," Daniel replied, moving to lend

any support Annabel might need as she levered herself out of the armchair. "Can you manage?" he asked, curling his arm around her waist, hugging her to his side.

She looked up gratefully. Her champion. "Thanks, Daniel. I'll manage. Go ahead with Neil. I want a last word with Izzie."

His expression hardened. "Time to walk away, Annabel," he murmured.

"I know," she answered, her eyes accepting the knowledge in his. "Go on. I'll be out in a minute."

Isabel, however, had nothing to say to her twin and no intention of being caught alone with her for an earful of recriminations or anything else. She went ahead of them, preceding them out of the house and down the path to open the front gate, then standing by the taxi while the luggage was loaded in.

She had done it her way—the payback for Annabel having the effrontery to ally herself with a man Isabel did not have the power to control. That was the trigger, Annabel realised, Daniel Wolfe's partnering himself with her and her own implicit desire for it. Ironically, his passion for truth had laid bare more hidden levels than Annabel had ever comprehended.

She didn't have much to say to her twin. Only one thing. She walked up to her, looked her straight in the eye and stated her position succinctly and decisively. "You're on your own, Isabel."

No affectionate diminutive of her name.

That feeling was gone forever.

The reply was just as succinct, just as decisive. "I don't need you, Annabel. I've got Neil."

So the bond of dependency was cut.

Annabel stepped into the taxi.

Daniel quickly joined her on the back seat.

The door was shut.

The relationship with her twin was irrevocably changed. She reached for Daniel's hand. It was warm and strong and comforting in this hour of emptiness.

CHAPTER SEVENTEEN

DANIEL had given the driver Annabel's address. There was no more he could do now except keep holding the hand that had reached for his. The taxi moved off into the night, taking them to the other side of the city, ringing down a welcome curtain of distance from the wretched denouement of Isabel's truth.

The cheating, lying, self-serving Judas had sold her twin down the river as fast as it suited her, no concern, no consideration, no loyalty, zero caring for her sister. And that after all Annabel had done for her!

It deeply offended Daniel's sense of justice to let her get away with it, but the prerogative for that decision belonged to Annabel, whose life he'd had to watch being smashed and redrawn as the helpless Isabel revealed herself as the ultimate survivor, prepared to destroy anyone to have everything arranged to her liking and advantage. No way in the world would that woman self-destruct. She had the coping capacity of a boa constrictor.

At least he'd been able to salvage something from the debacle, and by God! he'd make damned sure Jack Mitchell acted with integrity and kill a story that stood for nothing but needless spite.

He glanced achingly at Annabel, wanting more

than the physical bridge of her hand, but she sat beside him wrapped in a silence he didn't feel right about breaking.

He remembered how he'd felt the night he discovered Barry in Susan's apartment, shock waves sucking at his brain, robbing it of its ability to choose logical paths of thought or action, the sense of betrayal eating at his heart like some alien parasite that couldn't be detached, the soul sickness draining the energy needed to move past the pain.

He had no problem empathising with what Annabel was going through. It was probably far worse than he had experienced. His relationship with Susan had been of relatively short duration. Annabel had been closely involved with her twin since birth.

It must seem the world had changed. What she had believed all her life wasn't true, and facing the falseness of it brought an insidious humiliation. To be proved so wrong... The loss of faith in her own feelings had to cut deeply. The instinctive impulse, he knew, was to retreat from everything and shrink inside oneself.

Yet she had reached for his hand.

Daniel took great heart from that telling gesture. She didn't want to shut him out. Maybe she simply needed something to hang onto. Whatever...he was here for her. If ever there was an hour of need, this was it. He hoped she would let him share it.

Traffic was light. It wasn't long before the taxi was heading down the harbour tunnel and coming out on the northern side of the city. Another few minutes and they'd be at Annabel's apartment. Daniel decided to accompany her as a matter of course, not even ask if she wanted him with her. Why prompt a possibly negative decision?

Her fingers suddenly tightened around his. He turned his head to find her offering him a travesty of a smile. "I haven't thanked you," she said wryly.

"I wonder if we've become too civilised," he returned, intent on diverting her painful pattern of thought.

She looked puzzled.

"I sometimes think physical retribution could be very therapeutic. I really would have liked to box their ears," he confessed, hoping to lighten her mood. Laughter was the best medicine for many ills.

She sighed and turned her gaze away, staring out the side window. "I've often felt like that. But I always excused Izzie."

"Well, look at it this way," Daniel trotted out. "Now you can have the relief and pleasure of saying precisely what you think without feeling guilty about it."

She nodded, but her voice was flat and dull in reply. "Yes. That's one good thing. I'll never feel the guilt again." Another sigh. "I used to long for the freedom to be myself."

Daniel was reminded of the mother-in-law creeper in the Daintree Rainforest. Her twin had wound herself around Annabel, getting so many hooks in, it had probably needed tonight's savage surgery to get them out.

"I didn't realise it would make me feel so alone."

It pulled him up with a jolt. Easy to think of Isabel as a parasitical vine, clinging and digging into the tree strong enough to stand alone, but maybe Annabel had needed to feel needed by her twin. Such a long, close relationship had to generate a complex interweaving of personalities. Impossible for him to measure the emotional bonding.

"I'm sorry, Annabel," he said softly, acknowledging the loss, the sudden hole in her life.

Her fingers raked over his as the taxi slowed to a halt outside her apartment block. She shot him a glittering glance, her eyes moist with tears. "Stay with me?" she asked huskily.

He gave her a whimsical smile. "Of course. We're still on vacation."

It made her laugh, albeit a somewhat brittle sound. It took the tension out of the moment and made their exit from the taxi a relaxed affair. Collecting their luggage and paying off the driver was matter-of-fact business. Then Annabel was leading him to her apartment, hurrying as though she couldn't wait to get inside.

Wanting the security of the home she'd made for herself, Daniel thought, but he was wrong. They'd no sooner entered her living room and dropped their bags than she caught his hand and looked at him with eyes that sizzled with determination and desire.

"You promised me dessert."

He knew then. He knew she desperately needed the emptiness filled, and he was there for her if he was the man she thought he was. Daniel felt himself leap with eagerness, with a determination and desire to meet her every need. A wild joy kicked through his heart. She was free to move on with him. And she would. No weeping and wailing from Annabel Parker. She seized life as it was and dealt with it.

He grinned. "Something rich...treacle pudding and brandy custard." Very filling.

She raised a challenging eyebrow. "Can you deliver?"

The caveman stirred. *His woman*. He swept her off her feet, exulting in holding her against his chest, wanting to ravish all her senses until there was only him in her consciousness. "Direct me to the bedroom," he commanded. "Dessert should always be served in a comfortable place so one can linger over it."

"Door on the right in the hallway."

The instruction was punctuated by provocative kisses to the corners of his mouth. Fired by this incitement, Daniel burned a trail to her bed. There was no finesse in the discarding of their clothes. It was all pull, tug, drag and toss, a frenzy of action to get down to bare skin and the hot intimacy of naked flesh against flesh, rolling in it, revelling in it, tangling and entwining in a savage affirmation of intense togetherness.

Her wanton urgency begged fast fulfilment. He plunged himself into her, feeling the warm, convulsive ripples of ecstatic welcome. She used her hands and legs with a driving, uninhibited ardour to keep him coming, pumping the sensation to a nerve-screaming climax that could not be contained by either of them, spilling into an explosive meld of heat, fusing them to a moment of intense sharing. To Daniel it was a flow of love, uniting and bonding, and he fiercely hoped it was so to Annabel.

He started to relax.

She wound herself around him and rolled, coming up on top, holding him inside her. "I don't want this to end, Daniel," she said gruffly.

He knew she meant the togetherness. The physical expression of it was satisfying pleasure, but she meant much more than that. A huge slice of her life had ended tonight. If this came to nothing, as well...

"We've found more than I ever anticipated on our journey of discovery," she went on, her eyes deep whirlpools of emotion. "It hasn't all been good, but it's better knowing."

"Yes. It's better knowing," he agreed, aware she didn't want sweet words but bare truth. Decisions were being made in her mind. It was a critical time for her, and honesty was paramount. "As for our journey," he said with slow deliberation, "I think it could take the rest of our lives to experience everything we can together."

"Do you want to try?" Her body was tense, arched in a bow of proud independence.

"Very much."

"So do I," she said with a long sigh, leaning forward to hover over him in teasing invitation.

He smiled, sliding his hands up her body to cup her breasts, caressing them, matching his movements to the voluptuous sway of her hips. She made love to him and he made love to her long into the night.

He found her endlessly exciting, not just the touch and taste and feel of her, but in a far more deeply appealing sense, the mind and spirit and heart of her, all of them carrying the intrinsic essence of truth and the courage to face it and act on it, the strength, the power and the energy, such a bright flame burning within, shining through. It might be dimmed with shadows thrown by other people, but it refused to go out.

He loved her.

He adored her.

He cherished her.

When she finally snuggled up to him and sleepily whispered, "Enough, Daniel," the contentment in her voice told him her need had been answered. For now.

The hurt would come back when she woke in the morning. He couldn't make it go away. It would be a long time before Annabel came to accept viewing her twin differently, without a sense of loss.

But she wouldn't be alone.

She had given him her hand, and tomorrow he would put his ring on her third finger. Its superficial purpose was to show Jack Mitchell where the story was and cut Isabel completely out of it, which

Annabel had done from the beginning and Daniel was determined to do at the end. Consistency saved confusion.

The colour of the stone had not shown up in the photograph. He would buy Annabel a ruby ring, not an emerald. He would ask her to keep it on her hand as a token of trust in their journey together, to remind her she was not alone.

And never would be, if Daniel had his way.

CHAPTER EIGHTEEN

AYERS ROCK.

Uluru, the Aboriginals called it.

Annabel could well understand the spiritual significance it had for them. When she'd seen it at sunrise this morning, the huge monolith glowing in the desert like some great prehistoric beast pulsing with magical life, she'd been totally awed by it. Now, as she climbed closer and closer to the top, the sense of reaching something truly unforgettable was pounding through her heart.

"Are you still okay?" Daniel asked, following closely behind her to lend support in case she slipped or felt dizzy.

The rock had killed many people who had aspired to climb it.

She paused to throw him a reassuring smile. "I am not about to drop dead on my honeymoon."

He grinned. "Just checking. It would be a wicked shame if our journey was cut short."

And left one of us alone again.

He didn't say it, but she knew what was in his heart. It was almost a year since they'd met, and every day had been another revelation of how empty her life had been before him. What had she had? Izzie calling on her, making emotional demands, a career that exercised her mind and gave a kind of intellectual satisfaction that affirmed she was a person in her own right? She hadn't really wanted either. She'd wanted someone to know her and love her and make her feel whole, although she hadn't realised it until Daniel had shown her how it could be.

He'd done more than that. He'd given her himself, as well, no holding back on anything. The wonderful togetherness they'd discovered added so much to everything, it was like an extra shine to every pleasure and a warm blanket of comfort that covered even the smallest gaps between them, understanding, accepting, appreciating.

"This journey has no stop signs," she assured him, loving him for all he was, the deep inner caring of the man that always encompassed her, his passion for truth that generated a freedom she understood now, his determination to forge a path for them into the future.

She looked at the immediate path ahead of her and resolved not to falter. Steel posts had been hammered into the rock, and the chain linking them provided good support for tackling the steep gradient. Annabel hung firmly onto it as she started the final ascent to the top. She wanted to do this. She wanted to share it with Daniel.

The sunlight glinted on her engagement ring, striking a deep red fire in the pigeon-blood ruby. She smiled. It was a beautiful ring. Daniel had declared a ruby was the right gemstone for a woman who was beyond price, and she was certainly that to him. Even though she had initially worn it to settle Jack Mitchell's questions about the infamous photograph, Annabel had been happy to leave it on. It had felt good. She knew it always would, especially with the wedding ring accompanying it.

Bonds could be so different, she reflected, like chains, or a highway to heaven. With Daniel she could be truly herself, and he loved her as she was, no pressures, no obligations, pure happiness. Perhaps it was sharing the same values that made it so easy and natural. With Izzie, the bond had too often been more like bondage, though not any more, not since her perception of her sister had widened to take in another set of truths.

Steel and putty.

She shook her head over her false assumption that putty was weak. It wasn't. It simply had to be judged by different values to those attached to steel. Its properties were virtually the opposite. Putty went with the flow. It could adjust to anything. It could be rearranged to fit whatever the need of the moment was. It was flexible. Although it was shaped by outside forces and intrinsically mutable, putty was not to be considered useless. It might not stand by itself, but it could achieve surprisingly effective results.

Annabel no longer worried about her twin. Izzie was adept at finding a crutch when she wanted one. She really didn't need Annabel, although she still used her on occasion. In some ways they were closer because there was no longer any pretence involved. It was a different kind of affection. As Daniel had said about his tie of longevity and familiarity to Barry, who else knew all those years? In knowing, there was accepting. Family was family. That was bond enough.

Having reached the white-painted footsteps that heralded the last section of the climb, Annabel paused for breath, mentally measuring the remaining distance. Not far to go now, but the final few metres were tough, rising at about a sixty to seventy percent angle. One certainly needed the chain to hang onto.

It was a relief when she got over that hump, but they still weren't at the lookout point. It was quite a hike across the top of the rock, made very strenuous by deep striations, a series of ridges and valleys, some of which Annabel slid down on the seat of her jeans. So did Daniel. They laughed at each other, happy for it to be irrelevant how they got there as long as they did.

"Intrepid explorers like us will stop at nothing," Daniel declared.

"Not even holes in our pants," Annabel agreed, smiling over his words.

Intrepid explorers. It was Daniel who led the way. He had from the beginning, pushing, probing, pulling her after him. She loved him all the more for doing it, making her see what was possible, not letting her go. He was such a strong person, her husband, and Annabel knew she could always depend on him. It made her feel wonderfully secure.

At last they made it to the monument marking the ultimate place for them to reach, and the wind let them know there was nothing to block it, no protection here except what they gave to each other. Daniel stood behind Annabel, his arms wrapped tightly around her waist, her arms hugging his as she nestled against him.

It was the most amazing feeling, looking out at the rest of the world, the horizon seeming to revolve around them. It gave the eerie sense of being at the centre of the universe, a truly magical experience.

"It's like there's only us," Daniel murmured.

"Mmm. It's good we have each other."

They'd come such a long way, so far from that night when she had struck her pose of independence, saying she was on top of her world. She hadn't even known what her world was, not the truth of it. This was the top of the world, standing here with Daniel, bound together in a marriage so deep it went beyond formal vows.

The land, as far as the eye could see, looked as empty as it must have been when it was first created. It made Annabel feel as though she and Daniel were Adam and Eve. And soon they would make a family, children who would be loved themselves, no comparisons with others, no good-better-best, just children whom they'd encourage to explore the world around them at their own pace.

"Have I told you lately that I love you, Daniel?"

He rubbed his cheek over her hair. "Would needing me to hold you against the wind have something to do with this sudden affirmation?" he teased.

Yes, she needed him. It was a need that fulfilled her life, not a trap. Need, love... She sighed contentedly.

"I just want you to know that even up here, with all this around us, you are the centre of my universe."

"As you are mine, my love," he murmured.

So easy to say.

It was true.

For both of them.

AUTHOR NOTE

For most of us, the closest relationships we have are within our family—our parents, our siblings, our children. On the whole, they form the influences that drive our lives, shaping us into the people we are, for good or for ill. One's place—oldest child, youngest—will often dictate how we think, how we react and respond to situations and to other people. Yet, even within families, how well do we know each other? How much do we hide or suppress in trying to be what is expected or demanded of us? When are we truly ourselves?

In this story I have tried to portray this very human condition as vividly as it lived in my mind—Annabel's private desperation in the twin relationship with her sister, Isabel, and Daniel's struggles to come to terms with his older half-brother, Barry. Both Annabel and Daniel found themselves in the kind of crisis where people are driven to reveal their inner selves, where extreme pressure forces truths to come spilling out. For them—for all of us—only with knowing can real understanding grow. I hope you felt this, that you really knew and cared about the people by the end of the story, and that your journey with them was worthwhile and satisfying.

MIRA Books will soon be publishing my novel *The Secrets Within*. This story also revolves around family relationships; their strengths and weaknesses, loyalty, love and hatred, ambition and obsession, rejection and rebellion, betrayal and vengeance—every powerful force that family can and often does wield over its members.

The story deals with two long lines of heritage, lives and fortunes that have been interwoven for decades, for both good and ill. Under ever-mounting pressure from circumstances beyond the control of either family, the secrets are dragged out of hiding, one by one. You may be shocked as the truth unfolds, but you will see and recognize and understand the very human needs and emotions and passions that drive these people.

The Secrets Within is a much broader canvas, a darker, richer, more complex tapestry of lives than I've ever written before—a different journey, but also a compelling one, fascinating in its insights, heart-tugging in its emotional intensity. Nothing about this story is predictable, not even the end. I do promise you this, however…it is unforgettable.

Emma Darcy

HARLEQUIN PRESENTS®

**Psst. Pass it on...Harlequin Presents'
exciting new miniseries is here!**

Scandals!

You won't want to miss these scintillating stories
of surprising affairs:

September
SEDUCING THE ENEMY
by Emma Darcy (#1906)

October
A VERY PUBLIC AFFAIR
by Sally Wentworth (#1912)

November
MISTRESS OF THE GROOM
by Susan Napier (#1918)

December
THE RANCHER'S MISTRESS
by Kay Thorpe (#1924)

January
SCANDALOUS BRIDE
by Diana Hamilton (#1930)

February
RED-HOT AND RECKLESS
by Miranda Lee (#1936)

We've got your calendar booked!

Available wherever Harlequin books are sold.

HARLEQUIN ◆ PRESENTS®

Let passion lead the way, in our exciting series:

—when passion knows no reason...

Don't miss these dramatic stories about women who dare to risk it all for love.

August 1997—
DECEIVED (#1901)
by Sara Craven

September 1997—
THE HEAT OF PASSION (#1908)
by Lynne Graham

October 1997—
THE MARRIAGE WAR (#1913)
by Charlotte Lamb

Available wherever Harlequin books are sold.

The SECRETS WITHIN

The most unforgettable Australian saga since Colleen McCullough's *The Thorn Birds*

Eleanor—with invincible strength and ruthless determination she built Australia's Hunter Valley vineyards into an empire.

Tamara—the unloved child of ambition, a catalyst in a plan to destroy her own mother.

Rory—driven by shattered illusions and desires, he becomes a willing conspirator.

Louise—married to Rory, she will bargain with the devil for a chance at ultimate power.

Irene—dark and deadly, she turns fanatical dreams into reality.

Now Eleanor is dying, and in one final, vengeful act she wages a war on a battlefield she created— and with a family she was driven to control....

EMMA DARCY

Available in October 1997 at your favorite retail outlet.

MEDTSW